THIS TIME

A Time Travel Romance

M. S. MCCONNELL

To: Janice

Best

Mike McConnell

MSM Publishing

ISBN (Print) 979-8-9915502-0-8

ISBN (ebook) 979-8-9915502-1-5

Library of Congress Control Number: 2024919450

Printed in the United States of America

Book design by M. J. James Publishing www.mjjames.com

Prologue

July 2, 2026

THE PHONE ON the nightstand was vibrating audibly. *Bzzzt. Bzzzt. Bzzzt.*

He was asleep, dreaming of the nameless woman. *I think I'm… I'm so close, close enough to embrace her and kiss her exquisite shoulder. Behind her is darkness and shadow. But her shoulder…*

Bzzzt. Bzzzt. Bzzzt. Bzzzt. Bzzzt.

No. I want to dream. I want to touch—

Bzzzt. Bzzzt. Bzzzt. Bzzzt. Bzzzt.

He pulled himself out of his sleep and sat up, putting his feet on the carpet as he reached blindly for his iPhone, sliding his fingers along the edge of the nightstand until it was in his hand. Opening one eye, he saw "Unknown" displayed on the screen. He swiped right and sighed.

"He-hello," he mumbled. *Jeez, it's hot in here. I'm sweating. Did I turn off the A/C?*

"Jack?" A woman's voice.

"Yeah. Speaking."

"My name is Charlie, a virtual assistant. It's six a.m. A meeting has been deemed necessary to discuss the mission."

"Mm-hmm."

"Jack, please confirm that you understand. If you do, say 'yes' or press one."

"Yes. Mission." Jack cleared his throat. "Ahem. Yes, good to hear from you. I can assure you that I'm looking forward—"

"As always, Jack, do not discuss this with anyone. Not the mission, not the meeting, not this phone call. You will meet with Agent M in room two-oh-one in the One Eleven building on Craig Road. Please arrive at noon today."

"But—"

"Goodbye." *Beep.*

Jack lay back down on his queen-size bed dressed with white linens and pushed his face into one of the down pillows. Turning his head, he said, "Alexa, set alarm for eight a.m."

"Good morning, Jack. Alarm set for eight a.m.! Would you like to listen to an Audible selection?"

"Noo!"

Mmm. Who is the woman in my dream? I can always see her shoulder, her face, her neck, and her elaborately arranged hair. Her hair is styled back from that lovely face, and on the sides it's drawn back and up into a twirl at the crown, where the sections are woven into almost a knot from which ringlets fall. She's in profile, looking away. But mostly she's in shadow. The background is so dark. Nothing visible below her chest. It's like she's a ... cameo? Beautiful face, radiant alabaster skin, long eyelashes, the shoulders and neck of a princess or movie star... But a cameo. Ha! Cameo. A brief appearance, a single scene. Ain't that the truth. Beautiful women are great at making cameo appearances in my life.

At 11:54 a.m., Jack was just a block away from the twelve-story West Port Gold Tower, aka the 111 Building, an aging, mostly vacant commercial development a few miles west of St. Louis. He'd been instructed to meet yet again with a representative of a secret federal agency to discuss next steps in his years-long quest to be considered for the first manned mission to the planet Mars. Although Jack had never completely understood why they were considering a sixty-four-year-old man for a two-year crewed space expedition, he'd willingly and eagerly undergone the many hours of testing, the psych profile, the questionnaires, the physical endurance tests, the medical screening, and the background checks.

Jack drove into the lot, parking his white 2025 Chevy Trax in the row farthest from the entrance, an aisle of mostly empty spaces. He almost always took precautions like this to avoid dings and scratches. And while he really liked the Trax, the car did not excite him. Jack hadn't been excited about new car models since the 1980s; he hadn't been excited about much for a while.

As Jack walked across the lot toward the main

entrance, he noticed an attractive young woman (maybe thirty) in jeans and an army green T-shirt holding a smartphone and standing next to a fifteen-year-old blue Taurus. The message on her T-shirt was: MULTIPLE SCLEROSIS AWARENESS. The message that the car was silently communicating was *I'm not going anywhere.* One of the car's ancient tires was flat. The woman scrolled on her phone, looking down at the screen and frowning.

"Good morning," said Jack, slowing his stride for a moment. "Triple A on the way?"

She looked up for a second. "Oh, hi. No, I don't have that. I think I need to go to AutoZone and get Fix-a-flat. There's an AutoZone one point two miles away."

Jack stopped walking, closed his eyes, and sighed. He turned to her. "Yes. On Dorsett. Look, I'm running late for a meeting. Otherwise, I'd be happy—" He paused. "Do you not have a compact spare tire… a donut?"

"I didn't see it in the trunk."

"Did you look in the spare tire well?"

"The what?"

"Never mind. Here, let's take a look," he said. "Pop the trunk." She inserted her key, turned it, and the trunk creaked opened. Pushing away some fast food wrappers, jumper cables, and two romance novels, Jack lifted the floor liner. "There it is. It still has the installation instructions stickers. Probably never been used. That's good."

"I never knew it was there."

Jack understood instantly that this woman had never changed a tire. "I'll put it on for you. Okay?"

"Awesome."

He spent the next ten minutes removing the flat and

installing the spare, something he had done dozens of times since buying his first car in 1978.

After replacing the jack kit and putting the flat tire in the trunk, Jack said, "Be sure to get some new tires ASAP. You're not supposed to drive on the donut for more than sixty miles or so."

"Gotcha. Look, I really appreciate your help, mister. Can I buy you lunch?" The woman handed Jack some wet wipes. "Your hands are filthy. Very sorry."

Jack accepted the wipes and scrubbed his hands. "Like I said, I have a meeting. But I like your shirt."

She looked down at her chest. "You have a family member with multiple sclerosis?"

"No. Sorry. I meant the words. The letters in 'multiple sclerosis' are great for *Scrabble* or making anagrams. While I was changing your tire, I came up with two anagrams from the letters in 'multiple sclerosis': 'comeliest lip slurs,' and 'priceless limo slut.' Sorry about that last one."

She just stood there. Blinking.

"You drive safe now. Have a great day."

Jack took the main stairs two at a time to the second floor. He turned left and stepped toward the door to room 201. As he pressed down on the door's brass handle, he looked at his watch: 12:12. The room was dim (some light entered through the windows overlooking the parking lot) and completely empty save for two desk chairs near a window and an old man in a suit holding a briefcase. The man was very old. Gray hair. Gaunt. The room was warm and smelled of fresh paint and drying plaster.

"Mr. Jack O'Donnell! Please come in. I'm—"

"Sir, I'm sorry I'm late. There was a young lady outside—"

"I was watching as you as you crossed the parking lot. It's fine. You did a nice thing. That's one of the reasons why I like you." He extended his hand. "I'm Agent M." Jack shook his hand. "I must remind you that the mission is top secret, as I'm sure you know. Please have a seat."

Jack sat in one of the chairs. He looked at Agent M and then looked away. The man standing before him should be retired by now. *This guy doesn't look well. Mom died at age seventy-five. This man appears to be older than that.* "Yes. Of course. Top secret."

Agent M sat opposite Jack and opened the briefcase on his lap. He cleared his throat. "I have some forms and documents for you to sign. And I have a thumb drive for you."

"Wait. I've already—"

"Jack, you have been selected for a different mission," he said. "A different assignment. Mars, I'm told, is still a decade away. It's unlikely that NASA or SpaceX or any other foreign government or agency will be sending anyone to Mars who is over age forty. At least for a while. Your assignment is not with NASA, CNSA, or SpaceX, and, to be honest, it never has been. The department in charge of this program is classified. And officially…well, it doesn't exist. Do you wish to continue?"

Jack was silent for a moment. *I knew there was something off about this so-called mission. Going to Mars. What was I thinking! I'm an idiot.* "Yes, sir. But why—"

"Look, Jack, for a number of reasons, we couldn't tell you the nature of the mission until now. But we have been interested in you for a while. You are, frankly, perfect for this assignment. You have clearly shown a willingness to undertake a dangerous assignment. Your psychological profile and background tell us you are strong, honest, and resilient. And we have a dossier on you that shows you are trustworthy and mostly a loner. We know, for example, that you have never discussed the Mars program with anyone." Agent M smiled and stood. "Do you mind if I smoke?"

"Smoke?" said Jack. "Inside an office building in 2026? Go ahead. My mom smoked inside her house every day, even if it was seventy degrees and sunny outside. Smoked until the day we placed her in a nursing home."

Agent M retrieved a pack of Camel Filters from his suit coat pocket. He lit one with a Circle K lighter. "Your mom would have been eighty-seven today. Do I have that right?"

"How did you… Never mind. Yes. Today is her birthday."

"Jack, we've been monitoring your movements very closely. Since 2009 especially. We know you take care of yourself—bike riding almost every day. You eat healthy.

You learn new skills at an amazing speed. You've won writing contests. You excel at *Scrabble*. Your ability to write concisely and succinctly is quite impressive and a valuable talent. We also project, based on your current state of health, including your bloodwork, family history, and genetics testing, that you will live until age seventy-five, give or take. We'd like to begin cognitive testing on you in a few weeks. Further, if you agree to the parameters of the mission, you will be paid forty-five thousand dollars a year for the rest of your life. Direct deposit, of course."

Jack leaned forward. "Why cognitive testing?"

"I'll address that in a moment. But first, I want to tell you about your assignment. Over the next thirty days, we want you to compose a letter. It must be composed in Word in safe mode on a computer not attached to any network or the internet. You will save it as a .doc file and transfer it to a thumb drive and hand-deliver it to me in about one month—let's say August first—in this room. You will be contacted about the time. An edited version of this letter will be put in an email and transmitted to its recipient—you—by the end of August."

"Wait. What? I'm writing an email to . . . myself . . . me?"

"Yes, Jack. You can write mostly anything you want." He paused. "*Mostly.* However, we suggest that you stay away from saying too much about the current political situation. You know, the martial law, the arrests, and all of that. As I said earlier, we will be editing the letter, making redactions and…some annotations."

"I'm afraid I don't understand."

Agent M walked to the window and looked at the parking lot. He turned back to Jack. "We want you to write thirty-five hundred words (which is around thirty-five kilobytes of data) to your younger self. A brief memoir, you might say, of the last twenty-five years. We will be emailing this so-called 'memoir' to you in the past. If all goes as planned, Jack O'Donnell—you—will receive this email on December 31, 1999, when you are thirty-seven years old." He picked up a three-ring binder. He opened it and turned a page. "Let's see, in 1999—" he looked down for a moment "—you were the managing editor at a medical journal in downtown St. Louis. Salary: Forty-two K plus good benefits. 401(k). Dental. Recently divorced. Two daughters. You have a three-story fixer-upper in St. Charles, Missouri. From 1999 to 2009, you date a little—well, more than a little, right? You were a bit of a player. Is that fairly accurate, Jack?"

"Yeah."

"So, Jack, maybe write down what you've been up to since 1999. Give yourself career advice. Financial planning advice. Parenting advice. Dating advice. Maybe you can even avoid that second marriage. Am I right?!" He smiled. "But it's critical that you convince the recipient—you—that this email is from the future. If your younger self does not believe the email is authentic, the mission will not succeed. If it *does* succeed…well, Jack, you can change the future—your future. This is a wonderful gift we are offering you. And maybe, just maybe, you can create a life where Jack O'Donnell doesn't want to leave the planet in twenty-six years."

"Look, me wanting to get off this planet isn't just about my interpersonal relationships—"

"I know, Jack. We *all* know." Agent M sat again. "So, there are conditions and rules. And risks. You will not be allowed to transmit information that would assist your younger self in becoming an overnight millionaire, for example. No providing the names of horses that won the Kentucky Derby in 2000. Nothing about Super Bowl scores. You can't even send the winning numbers for Pick 3. And we are aware that your dad died in 2013. As you know, it's likely he would have lived much longer if he had gone to his doctor early in 2009 and had a mole removed. The melanoma. I'm afraid you cannot tell your younger self anything about that. I'm sorry."

Jack just stared at him. His dad had indeed died from an aggressive melanoma that metastasized to the brain. Will O'Donnell was the most decent man Jack had ever known. It had seemed so unfair to Jack that such a good man was struck down with that disease. And now it seemed unfair that he would be unable to change his dad's fate.

"Finally," said Agent M, "we need your younger self to contact two people in 2001 and persuade them to do something. Or, rather, *not* do something."

"Do I know them?"

"You do not. You have never met them. However, your younger self must persuade these persons to avoid air travel with United Airlines on September eleventh, 2001."

"Nine Eleven. Holy fuck!" *What am getting myself into?*

"Yes, 'Holy fuck.'" Agent M finished his cigarette and immediately lit another. In an attempt to be courteous, he blew the smoke toward the ceiling. "While we do not believe your younger self can stop the attacks, we think you can have an impact on some aspects of the very tragic events of that day. These individuals' lives must be spared. It's critical to national security, or so I'm told. Although I can't tell you much more, part of the email will include instructions to your younger self about how to persuade these men to travel a day or two early. Or by other means. Maybe drive. Take the train. A different airline. Let us worry about *those* instructions."

Jack sighed and shook his head. "So I can't save my dad. But you want me to save United Airlines passengers on Nine Eleven." He paused. "Why not have me contact the FBI or something before the attacks?"

"We don't think you—or anyone—can stop the attacks. If your younger self approached the FBI with stories of airplanes being hijacked on September eleventh—well, he would just get himself arrested and interrogated on September twelfth. Jack, we can't let your younger self be interrogated. It would jeopardize the program. Jack O'Donnell in 1999 will not be told anything about the events of Nine Eleven. He will simply be told to keep certain people from flying that day."

"If you can get email to *me* in 1999, you can certainly get email to someone at the FBI, right?"

"Jack, this is a new program. It's unknown exactly how this technology will affect current events. This is something of a test. And you are a guinea pig. As am I.

My contact with you can and likely will affect my timeline. It's thought that simply opening an email from the future will produce the butterfly effect. And of course if we succeed in keeping some passengers from flying on those doomed airplanes… well, we don't yet know the ramifications. It could be huge."

"And all of this will work? You're sure? You can send messages back in time?"

"That information is classified. Here, in 2026, we will continue to monitor you very closely. Once we send the email, we will check in with you to see if and how you are affected. If your younger self reads the email, believes it, and acts on it, it could have effects on your mental abilities and memories in the present, in 2026. Hence, the cognitive testing. There are other risks as well. But I'm not at liberty to go into details, I'm afraid. Some of the classified analysis is so sensitive that not even I have been briefed about it."

"If you are also a guinea pig, why do it?"

Agent M attempted a smile. Then he looked down at his hands. "I'm not risking much. I have lung cancer. This is my last rodeo. Maybe in *my* alternate timeline I won't be a dumbass chain smoker. And as for *your* alternate self, think George McFly in *Back to the Future.* Maybe in your revised timeline you will be more successful, happier, richer. Who knows?"

Jack thought for a moment. "I'm sorry about your cancer, sir. But why 1999? Why not a bit later?"

"Good question. Here is what I can tell you. A brilliant antivirus expert named McAtee wrote an app in late 1999. He'd been hired by America Online, or AOL, to make sure its email servers and chatrooms remained up and running when Y2K hit at midnight on New Year's Eve. However, unbeknownst to managers at AOL, or anybody else, this app had nothing to do with Y2K. It was designed to unscramble messages sent from the future. In theory, you see, messages sent to the past would be distorted by spacetime. According to his journal entries for December 31, 1999, the moment McAtee uploaded the app to AOL's servers and hit RUN, he received three emails. I've not been told what those emails said exactly. But they included instructions to delete the app.

"He took the computer offline and deleted the app immediately. The app had been live for around four and a half minutes. He then ran an antivirus program. A virus from the future could be difficult to detect and kill, he thought, so he went over the files personally. He deleted all suspicious code.

"It's thought that he never uploaded the program again. Most of his notes and code are gone—destroyed. But clearly, in 1999 he believed that those three emails were from himself. From the future. And clearly he believed the app was dangerous in the wrong hands. In late 2005, McAtee began to think that he was being followed. That his phone was tapped. So he disappeared. Some reports later said he had fled to South America."

Agent M paused and leaned forward. "So, Jack. Are you in?"

Jack looked back at this old man. "Look, sir, this is all a bit overwhelming. Honestly, I'm a bit disappointed that there is no Mars program for me. And I feel like a fool believing it for a second. I'm not a scientist, but even if I'm convinced that this is a real program and not some 'gotcha' TV show, there are things like temporal paradoxes that should make this unfeasible—or impossible." Jack paused. "I don't know. I need a few days to think about it."

Agent M lit another cigarette and inhaled deeply. "We are not sending you back to 1940 to kill your grandfather. We are sending thirty-five kilobytes of data to 1999. But you do raise a valid point. So the paradox you allude to may prevent us from sending the email. If that is the case, you have nothing to worry about. You will make a lot of money to write your thirty-five-hundred-word fantasy."

"I still want three days to think about it. Sir."

"Okay, Jack. I'll call you in seventy-two hours; let's say—" he looked at his watch "—thirteen hundred hours on Sunday. Okay? More details are in this packet, as well as the thumb drive." He tapped a 9 x 12 envelope and handed it to Jack. "If you decide to undertake this… adventure, you may relay some of these details to your younger self. To convince him that the email is genuine. However, do not share this with anyone else. Do not talk to anyone. You will return these documents to me on August first. Jack, I hope you decide to undertake this very important assignment."

Jack went home. As he walked into his living room, he stopped and admired his beautiful old house. He loved looking at the refinished hardwood floors, the stained-glass windows. As Jack walked into the kitchen, he opened the refrigerator and grabbed a Budweiser, twisted off the cap, and drank, savoring the taste with eyes closed. After a few moments, he walked out to the front porch, sat on the stone steps, and looked at the Catalpa Tree Coffee House across the street, remembering the evenings sitting with her on the ragged old couch there. Laughing. Talking. Listening to her sing. And Jack suddenly realized he had made his decision.

Jack's phone rang. The screen read "Unknown." He swiped right and put the call on speaker.

"Jack. Agent M here. I cannot let you have seventy-two hours. I'm afraid I need your answer by six p.m. this evening. Very sorry. My superiors insist on having your answer today."

"I have an answer for you now," Jack said, gazing at the coffeehouse across the street. "You see, I met a beautiful, gentle woman in December 2003. We were together for two months, and then she ended it. I didn't argue. I just left. My typical move. Three years ago, in 2023, I saw her for a moment in Colorado. And I realized the mistake I'd made twenty years earlier. Well, I guess I've always known that I'd made a mistake when I let her go. And so I want my younger self to meet her before December 2003 and to figure out how to stay in her life for more than two months. For more than two decades. Sir, if you agree to let me give my younger self directions on how to find her, I'll write the email and let you send it."

"One moment, Jack." Agent M put the call on hold. Thirty seconds later he was back on the line. "Jack. Yes. We have a deal. Congratulations! Go write that email."

Beep.

August 15, 2026

Jack was sitting on an exam table, fully clothed, in a temporary medical clinic in Ferguson, Missouri.

"Jack, thank you for coming in today. I'm Dr. Anand. I'm a retired physician who has been tasked with analyzing some tests you underwent this morning. Your cognitive test results are comparable with those from six months ago. You are healthy, and your brain functions are normal. Your thinking ability, your ability to learn and remember and solve problems, and other cognitive functions are appropriate and consistent with past measures. At this time, you have no impairments."

"Awesome. What a relief. I was told that my brain function could be affected."

"Well, hold on. The agency has not yet initiated the operation. I can assure you that the thirty-five-hundred-word message you composed has not yet been sent. That will happen in a few minutes. I want to make sure you wish to proceed."

"Do I have a choice?" Jack laughed.

Dr. Anand clapped his hands. "That's a good question. I hope you wish to continue because I personally do not have the power to stop it at this point. But I can pass along your request…"

"No. I'm good. Let's proceed."

"Splendid. If I detect any change in your speech or demeanor, we will send you out for some tests, including MRI, PET scan, et cetera."

"Fine."

"I'll be right back. Please lie down and make yourself comfortable."

Dr. Anand left the room. When he returned six minutes later, Jack was asleep on the examination table.

Dr. Anand walked across the room holding a clipboard. "Mr. O'Donnell! Please wake up. I need to ask you some questions."

O'Donnell opened his eyes. "Oh, okay."

Dr. Anand looked down at his notes. "Mr. O'Donnell, how do you feel?"

"I'm a bit tired. Probably a bit drunk."

"Really? You did not mention that earlier. And there is nothing in your history about alcoholism. Hmm. Mr. O'Donnell, what day is it?"

"January first. Happy New Year, sir!"

"I'm sorry. What did you say? I mean what is *today's* date?"

"January first, 2000. Saturday, I think… Where am I?"

"Mr. O'Donnell, this is quite extraordinary. I'd like to do a Rapid Cognitive Screen. Is that okay?"

Jack put a hand to his forehead and closed his eyes. "Ohh nnooo," he said as he slumped over.

Chapter One

December 31, 1999

I DECIDE TO STOP by The Amazon on Kingshighway to see if Shelly is bartending tonight. The bouncer is a big bear of a guy named Chop. "Hey, Jackie O! Happy New Year," he says.

"Hi, Chop. Happy New Year."

He waves me in before I reach for my wallet. It is fucking crowded tonight. And I suddenly feel old. Most of the patrons here tonight are in their twenties. I'll be thirty-eight in a few days.

I can see Shelly bartending at the main bar, but she is clearly very busy. I walk over in that direction, but she is too preoccupied to notice me standing behind several other thirsty patrons. My brand-new Tony Lama cowboy boots are sticking to the floor. They are brown leather, with a low-profile pointed toe and a western heel. And I love 'em. I wander over to the dancefloor and watch drunk people dance.

Shelly and I started dating several weeks ago. She is fun to go out with, but maybe a bit too high energy for me. When I turn back toward the bar, I can see her pouring shots for a group of four young guys. They are insisting that she take a shot, too. *Wonderful. She'll be fired if she's caught drinking on the job.*

At 11:59 and 30 seconds, the DJ begins the count-down to New Year's Day 2000. I think he has already played that Prince song two times since I walked in the door. A waitress named Cassie saunters over and hands me a Captain and Coke, saying, "Hey, Jack. This is from Shelly."

"Thanks, Cass." I drink, immediately realizing that it's mostly rum and just a splash of Coke. For me, Shelly pours with a heavy hand. I won't be finishing this drink.

"Three… two… one… Happy New Yearrr!" The DJ drops the needle on "Auld Lang Syne," and suddenly two small hands grab my face and pull me down into a deep, passionate kiss that tastes like margarita. But over-all, very nice.

The hands release me. Is it Shelly? Nope. A short blond woman, maybe late twenties, short hair, big earrings, says, "Happy New Year, gorgeous."

"Hi… you. Happy New Millennium!" I say.

"Huh?"

"I said happy…never mind. But thank you for trying to make sure that my New Year gets off to a great start." I turn and look over at the main bar and see that Shelly is leaning over the bar and kissing a young man in a leather jacket. I glance at my watch: 12:02. *Two minutes into the new millennium. Fuck. Really, Shelley? I hope he's a big tipper. You think I'm kissing those lips later?*

"Hey!" says the twentysomething blonde. "Hey! Hey!"

I turn back to the short blonde.

"Hi, you. Happy New Year," I say with no enthusiasm.

"Hey, are you okay to drive?" she asks.

"Yes. Absolutely."

"Ha! I'm not. Could you drive me and my friend to a party downtown? It's gonna be fuunnn."

I shake my head slowly. "Nope. But you have a great night. And a great year."

I turn and walk out of The Amazon.

I get home at 12:20 a.m. and decide to watch *Outer Limits* reruns, so I click on the TV. But I want to check email first. To see if the Y2K thing has wiped out my inbox.

I boot my computer and sign on with my AOL dial-up connection: *beep-BEEP-beep-BEEP-beep-beep-beep ppsh-hhkkkkk rrrrkakingkakingkaking- tshchchchchchchchcch*ding* ding*ding*pshhhkkkkkrrrrk-ping-pong-ping-pong-kahzzzzzzz-weeor-weeor-weeor…*

About three minutes later: *"Welcome. You've got mail!"*

My inbox is quite full. There are messages from Donna at work, the United Way, the Bicycle Fun Club, and Amazon (the huge online bookstore, not the bar). Then I see the following:

To: Jackodonnell3@aol.com
From: Jackodonnell3@aol.com
Subject: READ ME, JACK, YOU FUCKING IDIOT!!

I open the email and begin to read.

Jack, it's me. You. Twenty-six years in the future. August 2026.
You don't believe it. I get it. It's just spam, you say. You have come across this email perhaps a day or two after December 31, 1999. This email is in your Drafts folder or Inbox or maybe the Spam folder. I don't know. But you know that you didn't write it, so you think you might have been hacked. Change your password if it makes you feel better.

Okay, what is a "Spam folder"? And yeah, I think I will change passwords.

And you still don't believe me. So let's get to it.
Your first memory is Mom feeding Daniel cereal mixed with formula. Your first sexual experience was at seventeen with Trina in the apartment above the Laundromat. Your first alcoholic drink was a beer at Mom's second wedding, in 1978. In 1982, you lost your wallet in a nightclub in Iowa City. There was over $500 in it. You never told anyone. In early 1986, you had a brief fling with Belinda Carlisle.

WTF. Who sent this to me? No one person knows all of these things. In fact, only I know about the lost wallet. I get up and turn off the TV. I return to my IBM PC and read.

You believe me now. Right? If not, you will believe me next Friday, January 7, 2000. According to my journal, you will arrive to work at approximately 8:55 a.m. You will scan the hotel across the street for activity (like you do every day). You will see movement in room 1418. (And yes, I know you have memorized the room numbers on the east side of the Wyratt Hotel. You pervert.)

Seminude (wrapped in a white towel or robe), sipping from a coffee cup, she is standing at the window, watching the sun rise over the Arch. You are mesmerized. Minutes later, when you ring her room, telling her she is beautiful, she will hang up, but then, moments later, she will come back to the window and the towel (or robe) she is wearing will fall, letting you see her body. She will pose just inches from the glass. When you call back a few minutes later, she will agree to meet you for lunch. I remember that lunch very well.

I might be writing all of this for nothing. There is no guarantee that this message can be sent back in time. It sounds crazy to me, too. However, if all goes as planned, you will receive this on December 31, 1999. They tell me that it should arrive around 10 a.m. CST. ("They" are people from a government agency [I think] who have persuaded me to participate in this experiment. The compensation is very nice. I need the money.)

Apparently, a top secret program was created around 2008 to figure out how to send messages back in time to December 31, 1999. I do not know how many messages have been sent or will be sent—or to whom. The program was [redacted] when I met [redacted] in [redacted] [redacted]. [redacted] [redacted] At that time, all efforts to make this program work had been unsuccessful. Then last year (2025) someone put the question to AI (or artificial intelligence, essentially a technology that mimics human intelligence). The AI bot said it is possible. But all details are classified, so the public is not aware of this program. Further, messages can only be sent to December 31, 1999. Not December 30, 1999. Not January 1, 2000. Not even to 2025. There is just a four- or five-minute window on the last day of 1999.

I stop reading for a moment. This is definitely some Y2K bullshit. Email from the future? It's January 1, not April Fools' Day. But it is interesting, so I read on.

The app in 1999 that makes this possible was uploaded at AOL headquarters on December 31, and then uninstalled a few minutes later.

It is thought that sending messages back in time could be dangerous or unpredictable. And I don't know how dangerous this mission will be for you (or me). I don't know what to tell you to watch out for.

But it's safe to say that you may not be the only one receiving messages on December 31. Be careful.

I don't have much time or many words to send you. I'm forbidden to send photos or attachments or to say much about the current political situation.

There are many things humankind needs to know about the future. And if I could tell you, you likely wouldn't be surprised. And it is thought that you are powerless to affect any of the big events. In any case, no one will believe you, so don't go around telling people you have a message from the future. If certain people *did* believe you, you would be picked up and tortured. And then silenced. Further, I'm not allowed to send winning lottery numbers, the winners of the World Series, Super Bowl scores, best stocks to buy, et cetera.

At the end of this message you will find instructions from my "employer." They want you to contact some people and persuade them to change their travel plans on September 11, 2001.

[redacted] Other issues include the following:

On January 6, [redacted]

In November 2024, [redacted]

Again I stop reading. I don't understand why the

email has been redacted in so many places. Or why the big items are off-limits. I continue to read…

> It's unlikely you will be able to affect these events. But you can change yourself. You can be better. You can take a chance on a better life. You can touch the lives of others in a positive way. You should be kind and generous. You should listen and nurture.
> You are thirty-seven years old. I wish I could send a message to you in 1979. I would love to tell my seventeen-year-old self a thing or two. Be a better person. Less of a player. But getting to send a message to you in 1999 is not a bad deal.
> The advice I'm going to give you is not much different from advice that Dad or Mom might give you. Do you remember when Dad would check out a passerby and say, "Get back to yes"? By the way, in 2009, please make sure Dad does not buy that Uncle Moose car.

Wait. Dad said what? What the hell is he talking about? "Get back to yes"? Makes no sense. Uncle Moose?

> I can assure you I did not listen to Mom and Dad. But you should. You can be a better dad yourself. In 2026, your grown daughters are very successful in their careers. They are changing the world in their own ways. Both are still single.
> Make your kids your top priority every day. Spend time now. They will not stay in St. Louis after high school.

By the way, do not get remarried in 2009 or in any year that starts with a "2." Some men are not meant to be husbands. Read more. Study more. Take risks. Start a business. Throw away the TV.

I still live in Missouri. I'm sixty-four. Divorced three times. I'm still working. But recently, I thought I might be able to go to Mars (long story). I have some money in the bank but not enough to retire.

[redacted].

Jack, there is a book I like, *The Time Traveler's Wife*, about a man named Henry who could travel through time. Henry's wife was Clare, and his daughter was Alba. It came out in 2003, so I don't expect you to buy a copy anytime soon. And the movie came out in 2009. The last scene in the movie (which isn't in the book) was stuck in my head for a long time. And now that I'm writing to you, it has recently made me think about why it affected me so much when I saw the movie.

In the last scene, which is just over three minutes, Henry time travels into the future, to the meadow, and he sees his daughter, Alba, now age nine. (Henry had died when Alba was five.) Alba sees her dad and immediately sends her friends Max and Rosa to run to the house to get her mom.

Henry spends one minute and twenty seconds with Alba, telling her the story of how he and Clare met. Meanwhile, Clare runs through the meadow and into Henry's arms and spends fifty-nine seconds with him before he vanishes, apparently going back to the past. And so, I think, what would I give to have a minute or two with someone who is gone. Or maybe go back to a simpler time, a happier time. Maybe I'd go back to Joy's third birthday party (one of the happiest days ever), or go to Envie's high school graduation, or pop into Mom's house on the day after Thanksgiving, or return to Talladega with Dad.

You don't know this yet, but someday you may say that the job you loved the most was the job you had in the summer of 1980: a laborer at a cement plant. But this is not just about jobs and career choices. It's about living every day. Being with people you love and being grateful for each minute you are given in this world.

I can't go back to Joy's third birthday party. (And, well, neither can you.) But Envie's high school graduation ceremony is, for you, in twelve years (2012). So maybe this time show up *on time.*

I want you to buy a time capsule. Stainless steel. Large enough to hold a journal. If you can't find one, get a waterproof safe. Keep a journal for ten years and put it in the capsule. Paste in some pics of your kids. Newspaper articles. Whatever you feel is important during the first decade of the twenty-first century. And bury it underneath the tree. You know what tree I'm talking about.

Some things you can't change. Enjoy your thick head of hair while you can. Take care of your hair. Get it cut regularly and styled. Let your girlfriends enjoy your hair. Let them pull your hair. Ha! In 2007, it will start to fall like snow onto your page proofs. So enjoy it now.

The steady, unrelenting passage of time changes, Jack. It speeds up. My days are shorter now. The moon is full one day and seems to wane to a crescent in three or four days. At age sixty, a year is one-sixtieth of one's life. For me, summer seems to pass in a few weeks. Stop what you are doing. Go outside. Notice the azaleas. Consider how beautiful Ponderosa pine trees are. Contemplate for a minute the miracle of rain, of water, of ice.

Here are a few tasks that you should accomplish: According to my journal, on Monday, July 10, 2000, at 9 a.m., a woman was assaulted by a homeless man in her room at the Wyratt Hotel on Broadway. I saw it. It occurred on the east side of the hotel directly across from your office (the fourteenth or fifteenth floor). I've never gotten it out of my head. I tried to stop it, of course. I ran out of the office. I went to the elevator and waited almost two minutes. When the doors opened in the lobby, I ran across Broadway and into the hotel. But I was too late. But I believe you can stop it by simply calling the hotel manager on Sunday, July 9, and requesting that they increase security on Monday morning. So call. Talk to the manager. Tell him or her that you know that vagrants have been entering the building in the morning and harassing guests. Whatever. Then, Monday morning, arrive at the office around 8:50 a.m. and scan the fourteenth and fifteenth floors for the next twenty minutes or so. If you see a struggle, call the front desk and/or 9-1-1. Get security up to that floor. But do your best to prevent this attack.

[redacted]

Follow these instructions to the letter:

On Wednesday, October 2, 2002, at precisely 10:05 a.m., leave your office on the fourteenth floor. If you are questioned by Norma or your coworkers, tell them you are going to the ATM or the deli or something. Take the elevator to 4. Walk across the bridge to the parking garage. Head to your car (that morning you should drive to work and park on the green level). Retrieve a pair of tan vinyl gloves, tape, and a sign that reads OUT OF ORDER. Do not leave fingerprints on the sign or anything else.

Also, retrieve two large ROLLING suitcases from the trunk of your car (purchased at least a month earlier). Walk back to the bridge. The time should be around 10:14 or 10:15. If it is 10:16, pick up your pace. If it's earlier, walk a bit slower. Go to the elevator. Press UP. Go to the twelfth floor. Make a right and go to the east stairwell. Put on gloves. Carry the suitcases up to 13, the vacant floor. The lighting is dim. However, the bathrooms are available and accessible without a key. Go to the men's room on 13. Attach your sign to the door. Enter bathroom. Lock the door. The time

should be 10:18 or so. You have until 10:26 to leave the men's room. Take the suitcases with you.
When you leave, the bathroom should be completely empty. DO NOT FORGET TO TAKE THE SIGN WITH YOU. Take the cases to the stairwell and back down to 12. Call the elevator on 12. Take off gloves. Calmly get on the elevator with the cases. If others are riding with you, just nod a hello and press 4. Quickly exit the elevator on 4 and cross the bridge to the garage. (FYI, the security cameras you see on the bridge are dummies.)
Put the suitcases in the trunk of your car and calmly walk back to the bridge. Go back to your office. Work diligently for the rest of the day. At 5 p.m. put some work in your briefcase and head to your car. Exit the garage on Broadway and stop by the storage locker to drop off the suitcases. Be discreet. Be smart. Do not deviate from these instructions.

What the fuck is this about?

How did I get this opportunity to send a message back in time? I met someone [redacted].

More redactions. I stop reading. I need a break. To be honest, I'm fairly sure this is some fake bullshit… but I'll know more on January 7. I go to bed.

Chapter Two

January 7, 2000

I WAKE UP AT SIX THIRTY a.m. I shave and shower and brush my teeth, and then I sit in my outdated kitchen and eat old-fashioned oatmeal out of a ridiculously large JUAN VALDEZ coffee mug. I make a cup of pour-over coffee (Trader Joe's Dark Roast) with two tablespoons of almond milk. I didn't sleep well. And I don't know what to think. If the email I opened six days ago is from the future, I will have proof today. Then I will have to think about everything else that is in the letter.

I catch the MetroLink to downtown. I get off at the Busch Stadium station and walk two blocks to Broadway, carrying my briefcase and my Starbucks latte, which is no longer hot but still delicious. I step into my office at 8:52 a.m., close the door, walk to the window, and glance at room 1418, which is directly across the street from my office. The drapes are open, but the room is mostly in shadow. No movement. No seminude woman. Then, at 9:01, she's at the window, looking up and east, apparently at the Gateway Arch. This blond bombshell some seventy feet away from me is holding a white coffee cup and wearing a white bathrobe. The bathrobe is open in front, and I can see her amazing breasts and long legs. I'm already hard. And I suddenly realize that the email is authentic. It's from me…in the future. *What the fuck! It's true. Wait. It can't be. There is no such thing as sending messages to the past. I'm pretty fucking sure. But I just saw her. She was seminude. Looking east at the sunrise. Okay, I'm sure lots of tourists look east toward the Arch. People in hotels are often not dressed. I know that better than anyone. But I need to call her and see what happens.*

My office is in a building that is thirty years old: twenty-four stories of mirrored glass—two-way mirrors if you think about it. Many guests at the adjacent hotel apparently do not think this through. A twenty-four-story building covered in mirrored glass panels is *all* windows. In the mornings I can see into about thirty or forty rooms of the Wyratt. Most rooms are vacant by nine a.m. But not today.

I call the front desk and ask to be connected to room 1418. The clerk does not even hesitate. I can hear it ringing. The blonde turns from the window and walks toward the nightstand. She is in shadow now, so I can't really see her.

"Hello?"

"Good morning. My name is Jack." I pause for a moment. I feel like I can't breathe. "I know the St. Louis skyline is amazing in the morning, but not as amazing as you. You are unbelievable. A real beau—"

She hangs up.

In a few moments she is back at the window, the sun shining on her blond hair, but the robe has been cinched tight. She smiles. She sets down her cup. And then she unties the belt and lets the robe fall to the floor. Her pale skin is exposed to the gleaming Gateway Arch and the hundreds of workers here on the west side of the Equitable Building. She poses for a moment. Like a model. Then she simply stands there, not a stitch on, scanning my building with her right hand shielding her eyes, mostly looking directly across, as if she can see through the mirrored panels. And finally she turns her gaze to my office. I know she can't see me, but looking into her eyes is unnerving. The email nailed it.

She gazes at the Arch and the St. Louis skyline for maybe forty-five seconds. Then she turns and walks away.

I call back.

"Who is this?" she says.

"I told you. My name is Jack. I work in the building across the street. Thank you for that beautiful pose."

"Yes. Of course." She laughs.

"What is your name?"

"Valerie."

"Please tell me you are not checking out today."

"I'm in town until tomorrow," she says, "if that's any of your business."

"Great. I want to hear about how your trip is going

so far." I pause. "Let me take you to lunch today, Valerie."

There is a pause. "Maybe," she says.

"Joseph's restaurant is two blocks away. Kemoll's is three. I can meet you in the hotel lobby at eleven thirty. Does that work?"

"Well…"

"If you'd rather meet at the restaurant—"

"No…" She pauses. "Hmm. I'd rather you came up to my room at eleven."

"I would love that. I already have an appetite. I'd love to eat at eleven."

She laughs. "I like your voice. I just wish… I could see your face…"

"I understand," I say. "I'm thirty-seven years old. Five nine, one hundred ninety pounds, muscular in the upper body. Brown hair, clean-shaven."

"Okay, but maybe I shouldn't…maybe we shouldn't—"

"Valerie?" I interrupt. "It's nine fifteen. I can be at your room in five minutes. And then you can see what I look like. And I would love to meet you."

She giggles. "Well, I haven't showered."

"Please do not shower."

"I see. Okay. I'm in room—"

"Sweetheart, I know your room number."

"Oh, right. See you in five, then." She hangs up the phone, comes back to the window, blows a kiss to the St. Louis skyline, and closes the curtains.

I grab my Tic Tacs from my desk and head to the

front desk and tell Nikki that I forgot about my dentist appointment.

"I should be back in about an hour," I say. "I have to run."

I return to the office two hours later. I step briskly into the office, and Nikki gives me a look that includes rolling her eyes. "Norma was looking for you ten minutes ago—"

"Sorry, Nikki," I say. "Traffic was crazy. And I had a… uh… cavity filled. My tongue is still numb."

Norma is the executive director. She's mostly hands off when it comes to my department, but she certainly noticed that I was out of the office for two hours.

My tongue may be numb, but I've had a great morning. And I am so stoked about getting information from the future. I can't wait to get back to the email. *This is crazy! What other gifts are in that email?*

Chapter Three

January 8, 2000

IT'S SIX P.M. I'm in my living room, on my hands and knees, running my belt sander across the hardwood floor, occasionally getting up to have a sip of beer and peek out the blinds, wondering if my life is being monitored. Wondering if this is an elaborate joke. I'm not sure that it's possible to send a message even one millisecond back in time. But twenty-six years? It seems so fantastic.

I finished reading the email yesterday when I got home. The tryst with Valerie was fun. But was it a setup? I can't get Valerie or the email out of my head. The rest of the email reads as follows:

> Lastly, I met a woman in a chatroom in late December 2003. Anna Connor. We had a brief romantic relationship. She ended it less than two

months later, the day after Valentine's Day. My pride prevented me from trying to change her mind. I simply walked out of her house and never called her again.

Jack, she is fucking beautiful. Inside and out. Pristine blue eyes and a tongue that mesmerizes. Her heart is true and loving. The way she looked into my eyes has never left me.

If you can stop being a player and get over your so-called insecurities, I want you to meet her several months *before* December 2003. In the spring or earlier. She was working at the Granite City Walmart in December when I met her. (She also did some singing. Mostly karaoke, but also some gigs at cafés and clubs. Her voice is amazing.) Soon after meeting her I found out she was also dating a guy whose first name was Tom. In fact, he was her fiancé. Anyway, despite taking precautions, Tom and Anna got pregnant in the late summer or early fall of 2003. In October or November, Tom persuaded Anna to get an abortion at Planned Parenthood in East St. Louis. This was done to keep Tom's strict Catholic parents from knowing that Tom and Anna were having sex before marriage.

The abortion devastated her. When I met her, just after Christmas, she was overwhelmed with guilt. Her smoking had gone from one to two packs a day.

After our thing ended, she married Tom. They then had two kids—boys. Eventually, she left him and took the kids.

So again, I want you to meet her before she meets

Tom. I think she will date you. Be good to her. Consider that, for me, she is the one who got away. If she gets away from you, you will regret it. However, if she does rebuff you, at the very least persuade her to be careful. If she's with Tom, ask her to make sure the fiancé is using condoms. And maybe she needs to go on birth control as an extra precaution. Anna lived on Idaho Street in Granite City. I often thought about contacting her. And in 2014, after my second divorce, I tried, but I learned she was still married.

In 2023, I traveled out west to visit daughter Envie. We were having dinner at the highest elevation restaurant in Colorado—Alpino Vino. Located in Telluride. We were having wine and dessert when I saw her. Anna was being seated across the room, and she was with a man. Our eyes met for a moment. And then, about every two or three minutes, I would look up and watch her for a moment. After a while, I decided to order another glass of wine, and as I looked around for our waitress, I noticed that Anna was not at her table. But the man, her companion, was still sitting at their table, facing away from me and apparently scrolling on his phone.

I assumed Anna had gone to the ladies' room. So I stood up. I told Envie to order another Zinfandel for me. That I would be right back.

I made my way to the restrooms and nervously lingered outside the ladies' room. A minute later, she walked out...

"Anna," I said. "It's good to see you. And such a surprise. I never thought I would see you again.

Certainly not a thousand miles from St. Louis. It's been almost twenty years."

"Jack, it's good to see you. But I can't—"

"Got it. I know you are with someone—"

"He's my husband."

"All right. I just wanted to... well, to say..." I look over my shoulder for a moment. We are in a short hallway and shielded from the dining room by a wall. I turn back and look at her eyes, her mouth, her cheeks. "Look, I know I'll never see you again. But may I hold your hand for just thirty seconds? Then I'll go back to my table, finish my wine, and—"

"Is that your daughter?"

"Yes."

Anna stepped closer. "She's beautiful." And then she grabbed my hand. "Jack, kiss me one last time. And then look into my eyes."

And we kissed. I tried to note every sensation, every sound, every breath, every taste, every scent. And I touched her face, which was smooth and soft. The entire kiss lasted forty or forty-five seconds. And then she pulled away and looked into my eyes expectantly. I looked into her eyes and saw something like longing and regret and maybe sadness. What she saw in mine... well...

"The look in your eyes hasn't changed, Jack. You can't hide it."

I could not speak. For years I'd fallen asleep knowing I would dream of her. Then years of trying not to dream of her. How stupid is that?

"Jack, I got your 'thank-you card' in 2009. I quote:

'Ms. Connor, Thank you for your $5 donation to the Down Syndrome Association. Sincerely, Mr. Billy E. Mouere.' That was you, right?"

"Yes."

"I figured out the anagram, *'Mr. Billy E. Mouere.'* It took me a while."

"I just—"

"Me too, Jack."

And she turned and walked away. For good.

Then I realized she had left something in my hand. I looked down and opened my palm. There in my hand was a gold earring in the shape of a butterfly.

Jack, I know you have been hurt. Your heart has been broken over and over. But Anna will not break your heart. Yes, in 2004 Anna and I broke each other's hearts. But I could have fixed it. Unless you can see what can be, you will simply be a second-class player who never finds true love.

Jack, July 2026

[Jack. My name is Agent M. I am your employer in 2026. As you may have noticed, we have redacted some text from the letter above. This includes any information that has been deemed dangerous, unethical, or that could be counterproductive to the mission. In the spirit of transparency, we have shown you exactly how much of the letter was redacted.

This email has been sent to you with conditions.

One, do not tell anyone about this message.

Two, do not attempt to reply to or forward this email.

If you need a copy of the text, copy and paste the text into a Word-Perfect document. Print it out. Then delete the file as well as the email.

Three, we need you to contact Todd Beamer (b. November 24, 1968; ph. 848-555-6793; 17 Short Hills Circle, Milburn, NJ 07041) and Mark Kendall Bingham (b. May 22, 1970; ph. 201-555-1919; 1555 Netherwood Dr., North Plainfield NJ 07062). In September 2001, they intend to travel by plane to the West Coast from New Jersey. Call them from a payphone in the summer of 2001. The payphone should be at least one hour's drive from your home. Do not meet them in person. Do not tell them your real name or where you are located. Persuade these two men to avoid air travel on September 11, 2001. They can travel by plane any other day. September 10. Or September 9. Pay them a few hundred dollars in cash if that works. Just no air travel on the 11th. If they must travel by air on September 11, they should use JetBlue or Delta or American Airlines. Just not United. If you succeed, it will accomplish a few things, none of which I am at liberty to discuss. But you will be rewarded. Good luck.]

I believe the email is authentic. I do. And I trust the author (me) in 2026. But do I trust Agent M? I do not. If they can send email to me, they can send email to almost anyone. It is possible that I am or will be monitored and followed. I have several assignments coming up. I need to commit the email to memory.

I stop sanding the floors. I decide to run some

errands—maybe eat dinner at Denny's, stop by Dollar General, go to the ATM at the bank. I need to know if I'm being tailed.

I head out my back door, get in my car, and head to Denny's. I don't see anything suspicious on my drive or at Denny's. After my dinner, I pick up bleach and bottled water at DG, then head to the bank. The ATM at Bank of America on Fifth Street is a walk-up. As I enter my PIN, I see a silver car, maybe a Prius, pull up to the curb across the street. The windows are tinted, so can't see the driver. As I glance at the car, it pulls away from the curb and drives south on Fifth Street. I walk back to my car and head to Mobil for gas.

At Mobil, I insert my credit card into the card reader. The screen reads: *CAR WASH TODAY?* I press NO. *RECEIPT?* I press NO. *LIFT HANDLE AND SELECT GRADE.* I grab the pump handle and press Regular. I lean against my car and watch the pump as the screen ticks off the fuel being dispensed in thousandths of a gallon. It's just a blur. In my peripheral vision, I see a silver Prius two pumps over. I keep looking at my pump display. It shuts off with a clunk. The screen reads: 10.256 gallons. Price: $16.40. *Holy crap, gas is expensive.*

I get in my car, turn the key, and drive home.

Chapter Four

July 10, 2000

ACCORDING TO THE EMAIL, this is the day that a woman was attacked in her hotel room across from my office. Today should provide proof that I can change the past and affect the future. Yesterday, I called the hotel and spoke to the manager. She assured me that she would increase security in the lobby and make sure that transients and non-guests would be escorted from the building.

I walk into my office at 8:55, close the door, set my briefcase on the desk, and take a sip of my caramel macchiato. I walk to the window overlooking Broadway and scan the high-rise Wyratt Hotel for activity. Typically, by nine a.m. on a Monday, most hotel guests have already left their rooms. Open curtains typically reveal vacancies with unmade beds. Other rooms are shielded with closed curtains or are obscured by the shadow of my building. Sometimes, usually in the afternoon, I can see children jumping on beds or standing on the windowsills, faces pressed to the windows.

At 9:02, I see movement. A white man, long brown hair (dreads maybe), beard, plaid shirt, is pushing a woman to the bed, violently pulling off her robe.

"No. No," I whisper. "No. This shouldn't be happening." *I called the manager yesterday.* I'm suddenly lightheaded, almost fainting. I slap myself.

He turns her over, holding her arms behind her, thrusting violently, madly. She struggles against him, screaming (I think), shaking her head wildly, long red hair whipping back and forth. Then apparently giving up or going into shock, she goes limp. The rapist is unfazed. His rhythm does not change. I look down and begin counting from the concrete patio on the third floor. "Three, four, five," I whisper. "Six, seven, eight, nine, ten, eleven, twelve, fourteen, fifteen . . ." Then I count over from the left: "Fifteen sixteen, fifteen seventeen, fifteen eighteen." *Room 1518. Oh my god.*

I pick up the phone on my desk. I dial 9-1-1.

"Emergency nine-one-one. What is your emergency?" The voice is female. Raspy voice. A smoker. She seems irritated, so I freeze. She speaks again, this time putting a stress on the word is. "What *IS* your emergency?"

"Yes. He-hello. A wo-woman is being ra-raped at the Wyratt Hotel on Br-broadway. Fi-fifteenth floor."

"Sir, how do you know this? Are you a guest at the hotel?"

I pause again. *Why am I stuttering?* "I-I can see it from my office across the street. Please se-send the police."

"Okay. Let me understand this. You can see a couple having sex in a *hotel,* and you believe it's against the woman's consent?" She was clearly unconvinced, dismissing me, now even more irritated.

"Yes. Yes! She was screaming, I think, and fighting him. She has gone limp now. But she is still being assaulted. Right now." I look back at room 1518. He continues to hammer his body into hers. "Please hurry. This is not a joke." I think that I am sounding like a rational person, but I feel helpless, desperate.

"Sir, how can you—"

I hang up the phone. I call 9-1-1 again, praying for a different dispatcher.

"Hello!? Did you just hang up on me!?"

"I need to speak to someone who will send the police to stop a violent attack—a rape. If you won't do it, I'll go over there myself. So you'll need to send the police to stop me from committing a battery on a man with a beard who is raping a woman on the fifteenth floor of the Wyratt."

"Hold please." She puts me on hold, probably for a few seconds, but it feels so much longer. "Sir, officers are en route. What is your—"

I hang up. It's now 9:06 a.m. I don't know what to do. I reach for my binoculars. *Should I call the front desk? Should I go to her room? How long will it take the police to get to her? Five minutes? Six? Will the police call me back? Yes, you idiot, they will be calling. I'm a witness, for Christ sakes.* I put the binoculars to my face. At 7x magnification, the scene is sickening. *Oh my god. They will want to know how I knew the floor. Shit. They will want to know how I know there is no thirteenth floor. Should I have told them the room number?*

I speed-dial the hotel. Maybe the man will leave if the phone rings in the room.

"Wyratt at Busch Stadium. Front desk. Brad speaking. How can I help you?"

"Room fifteen eighteen please," I say, panting. "Hurry."

"What is the name of the guest you wish to speak to, sir?"

"Please just ring the room!"

"Sir, for security reasons, I must insist—"

"Security!? If you had decent security, a woman would not be getting raped in her room this very minute. Send your so-called security to room fifteen eighteen immediately. By the way, police are on the way."

Click.

I hang up on Brad.

9:13 a.m. A police cruiser, with the overhead lights flashing red and blue, is double parked in front of the twenty-two-story Wyratt Hotel in downtown St. Louis. From my office, I can see two tiny figures in blue emerge from the car and walk with purposeful strides toward the entrance. The officers disappear into the hotel lobby. I raise my head and look into her room, less than eighty feet away. She is still lying on the bed, nude and in a fetal position. The man is gone. My hands are shaking. I lower the binoculars. *Why didn't security prevent this? I called. I warned them.*

At 9:18 a.m. a male police officer is standing at the window of room 1518. He is perhaps looking at his reflection in my office window. I know he can't see me. Soon, he looks up and east, then down at the traffic, then over his shoulder at the woman on the bed. A female officer and EMS workers are tending to her. The male officer closes the drapes.

Somehow I get through the day. I lay out several journal articles and audit the printing invoice from last month.

I pick up my girls from their afterschool program and take them to dinner. Tonight it's Dairy Queen, the one on Dorsett that lets us watch Nickelodeon on the TV in the dining area. We eat chicken baskets and ice cream and watch an episode of *SpongeBob* called "Free Balloon Day." In this episode, SpongeBob and Patrick "borrow" a balloon from a vendor's cart, and as they talk about the things they plan to do with it ("First, we can RUN with the balloon!"), it suddenly pops. Realizing that they can no longer return the balloon, they conclude that they've now stolen it. When they bump into the owner of the balloon cart, they run away before he can tell them that it is Free Balloon Day. They decide to skip town, believing that they are wanted criminals. *What a coincidence. I believe I'm a wanted criminal, too.*

After Dairy Queen, I drop the girls off at their mom's house. I head home.

I turn on the TV at ten p.m. and pace my living

room. St. Louis TV news anchor Karen Floss is reading from her teleprompter. I met Ms. Floss once, at Six Flags. Floss has an hourglass figure. Amazing. But sitting behind her anchor desk, on TV, you would never know.

"In other news, St. Louis police report that a female guest at the Wyratt Hotel on Broadway was raped by a homeless man in her room this morning around nine a.m. A spokesperson for the St. Louis Police Department tells NewsChannel Five that the alleged rapist walked into the South Broadway hotel early this morning, rode the elevator to the fifteenth floor, wandered around knocking on doors, and eventually knocked on the victim's door. The man claimed to be from the housekeeping department. When the victim opened her door, the man forced himself in and attacked her. The victim's screams went unanswered apparently because all other guests on that floor had checked out by that time. After the attack, the assailant took the victim's purse and fled. Hotel security, noticing an unkempt man with a purse, apprehended Anthony Dubbus, age thirty-seven, as he tried to exit the hotel. A hotel manager notified police. Neither the police nor the Wyratt are releasing the name of the victim. A spokesperson for the Wyratt Hotel chain says plans have been underway for almost a year to make elevators at all Wyratt properties more secure and accessible only to guests with a key card."

Okay. So the Wyratt is taking credit for catching the rapist. A "hotel manager" contacted police?

So, will I get a call from police? Will I be interviewed? Arrested? I should be fine, right? They caught the guy. A good citizen saw it play out and called police. I certainly can't be implicated in a rape, right. Shit. My relationship with my ex-wife is really good. I get to see my girls three days a week, fifty-two weeks of the year. But if I'm implicated in a rape or being a peeping Tom? Fuck me.

I go to bed. But sleep is elusive. I get up and pace my bedroom.

That poor woman. My future self warned me to stop the attack on that woman. I had one job today, and I failed. I will never get it out of head. So terrible. Why has it affected me like this? Triggered me? It wasn't my fault. I was seventy feet away. I've never witnessed anything like that… Well, that's not true, is it? When I was fifteen or sixteen, I once heard muffled screams and slaps through my bedroom wall. But I dismissed it as none of my business. I told myself that I really didn't understand what I was hearing. It was just passionate. A bit rough. I didn't SEE it, though. Now I have. Christ.

Chapter Five

July 11, 2000

I'M SITTING AT MY DESK at work, trying to proofread articles for the journal. I can't seem to concentrate.

Nikki buzzes me. "Jack. Call on line one."

I pick up. "Jack O'Donnell. How can I help you?"

"Mr. O'Donnell. I'm Detective Nocchio, St. Louis Police Department. Is this a bad time?"

"Well—"

"Great. I'll keep this brief. Did you make a nine-one-one call yesterday about a battery that allegedly occurred at the Wyratt on Broadway?"

Did he say "allegedly"? "Well, to be honest—"

"Mr. O'Donnell. Your company's phone number was logged by the nine-one-one system yesterday. A few minutes ago, I called that number and talked to Nikki, the receptionist in your office. I said, 'Good morning, this is Detective Nocchio with the St. Louis Police Department. Do any of your employees have a clear view of the Wyratt Hotel across the street?' You know what she said? She said, 'Well, Jack O'Donnell's office is on that side. He can see the Wyratt. Is there a problem?' I told Nikki that there is no problem. I just want to ask Mr. O'Donnell some questions. So Jack, would you mind coming down to the station this morning? We have some questions. It's not a big deal. We are just following up."

"Following up on what?"

"Please, Mr. O'Donnell. Let's say eleven a.m.? Ask for me when you arrive."

"Sure." *Click.*

I decide to head to the water cooler. I see Nikki at her desk, so I make a detour.

"Look, Nikki—"

"Jack, I don't even want to know. Okay? And Norma will not hear it from me."

"Awesome," I say solemnly. "I'm going out for lunch today."

"All right."

I get a cab on Broadway.

"Where to, buddy?" says the driver. This guy is wearing ten times the recommended amount of cologne. *What kind of funk is he trying to cover up?*

"The police station on Clark Street."

"You got it."

The cab pulls over to the curb. I toss ten dollars at Mr. Old Spice and get out. I walk briskly toward the station. Once inside, I give the desk clerk my name and I'm led into a windowless room on the second floor. Walls are painted light blue. Mirror on one wall (clearly a two-way mirror). A nondescript security camera is mounted high up in one corner of the room. I sit on a wood chair and place my hands on the table in front of me. The security camera seems to be pointed at me. *I hope they're watching me,* I think. Then I realize I'm thinking what Norman Bates was thinking in the final scene of *Psycho.* I giggle.

Two male officers walk in after I've been sitting there for ten minutes. The larger one is holding a three-ring binder. He closes the door, then says, "Mr. O'Donnell, I'm Detective Nocchio. This is Officer Harris. Please tell us what happened yesterday morning."

"Well, Officer, I got on the train around—"

"Mr. O'Donnell. Please. We don't care about your train ride. Let's start with events that began around nine a.m."

"Yes, of course," I say. "I had just arrived at work. I think I had my coffee, or latte, in my hand as I closed the door to my office. I turned toward the windows on the west side of my office, which overlook the hotel, and I saw movement in one of the rooms. It appeared to be a rape. Well, I'm sure it was a rape. He smacked the woman, pushed her down... So I called nine-one-one and asked the operator to send help."

The officers don't say anything. They just stand there, mute. They want me to keep talking. But I don't know how much they know. So I decide to remain silent, too, and after about two minutes Nocchio steps forward, sits in a chair, sets the binder on the table, and says, "Yes. We have transcripts of *both* of your calls." He opens the binder and reads for a moment. "You said the battery was occurring on fifteen. The fifteenth floor. You saw a couple engaged in sexual activity from seventy-seven feet away—we measured it—and determined immediately that it was a battery? Is that correct?"

"First of all, I said 'rape.' That's what I said when I called. You calling it a 'battery' makes it sound less serious and—"

"Mr. O'Donnell, sexual battery is a felony. It is serious. Please continue."

"Okay, yeah. I was estimating the floor, of course. My office is on the fourteenth floor. Once I saw him pushing her, I did pull my binoculars from my desk to verify that it was an attack."

"Binoculars? In your desk? At work? In your office that is across from a hotel? Interesting. Well, Brad, the front desk attendant, says he received a call around 9:07 a.m. He said a man called and wanted him to ring room fifteen eighteen. When he asked for the guest's name, the caller told him about the attack. Brad did send security to that floor immediately. And we certainly appreciate citizens calling the police to report suspicious activity."

I could feel my heart beating in my chest. "It was more than suspicious. I watched a violent rape. I think I'm going to have nightmares for a very long time. It was sickening. I have daughters, Officer Nocchio. I worry about a world where a woman is not safe even in a luxury hotel."

"The rape did, in fact, occur in room fifteen eighteen," says Nocchio. "Mr. O'Donnell, do you have the rooms of the hotel memorized? Do you know the room numbers, somehow, of the windows that face Broadway?"

"Look, yes, I know the room numbers on fourteen and fifteen, as well as twelve and eleven. I can't see much below eleven."

"So, then, you know that the Wyratt does not have a thirteenth floor?"

"Yes."

"We sent a detective to the fourteenth floor of your building early this morning. He reported that he could see clearly into the Wyratt Hotel's rooms on fourteen, fifteen, sixteen, as well as twelve, eleven, ten, nine, and he could even see the beds near the windows on eight."

I look down at my hands. Then look directly at Officer Nocchio. "Okay, so sometimes if I see an interesting person, I pick up the phone and ask for their room. It's not very often. But I just strike up a conversation."

"Sounds a little weird, to be honest, Mr. O'Donnell. Suspicious even. I suspect you have scared some of the guests of the Wyratt. Would that be a fair statement?"

"Look, did I do something wrong?"

The detective is silent for a moment. "I'm not sure." He stares at me. "We do not think that you have any connection to the rapist. Anthony, the suspect, normally panhandles over on Olive in front of a Chinese restaurant. Now he's going to prison." He pauses, clearly wanting to ask me another question. And he does. "A woman named Debbie works at the Wyratt. She's the general manager. Do you remember talking to her on Sunday?"

"No," I lie.

"A man called Sunday and advised her to, quote, 'increase security' in the lobby on Monday. The caller said that transients were entering the building in the mornings and harassing guests."

"Wow. What a coincidence. Sounds like Debbie dropped the ball. There should be a lawsuit."

The officers look at each other. The detective sighs.

"Mr. O'Donnell," says Detective Nocchio, "you are free to go. We ask that you not call the Wyratt unless you are booking a room. And as a favor to me, do not talk to the news media about this … incident."

"Gotcha. Yes, sir."

I head back to the office. My hands are shaking. And I have to pee. I think I've dodged a bullet, but I'm still worried. *Jeez, what is wrong with me? The officer is right. Knowing the room numbers is weird and creepy. I'm taking the binoculars home. No more calls. No more peeping.*

At four p.m., Nikki buzzes me. "Jack, you have a call on one. She says her name is Apollo. It's about an email you received in December."

"Thanks, Nikki."

I pick up the receiver.

"Hello. Jack O'Donnell."

"Jack, my name is Apollo." The voice is young-sounding. Maybe twenties or early thirties. "I'm going to make this brief. You received instructions from an Agent M on December 31. Do you recall that?"

"Yes."

"Well, I, too, received an email on that day," says Apollo. "And it contains a message for you. It says that it is possible that you will be approached or called and told to ignore those instructions. Agent M wants you to know that that would be a mistake. You must contact Mr. Beamer and Mr. Bingham. Do you understand?"

"Yes. Hey, Apollo, we should stay in touch. It is so weird that—"

"Stop talking. I'm not finished. You were given the okay to contact Anna. Do you remember that part of the email?"

"Yes, of course."

"You are now instructed to not make contact with her until late December 2003. Do you understand?"

"Yes, but—"

Click.

Okay. So apparently there is a battle. Some people want my mission to succeed. Others want to stop it. And I don't even understand what will be accomplished if I keep these guys off the plane. My future self agreed to this assignment. But what if my actions create an unforeseen chain of events?

And Anna. If I wait until December, the procedure will have already been done. She will be damaged. Heartbroken.

Chapter Six

August 4, 2001

IT'S SATURDAY. I wake up early. I have a quick shower, get dressed, and eat a toasted bagel with cream cheese and jam. I mow the lawn.

I've finally decided to contact Todd Beamer and Mark Kendall Bingham. There have no further calls from Apollo or anyone else, but I've thought about this day for a long time. My future self was allowed to send an email to me if he agreed that I would be instructed to make some phone calls and keep two men off a plane. It's odd. But there is nothing about this assignment that feels wrong or dangerous. Just... unusual. Paying someone not to fly does not sound illegal or immoral to me. It certainly sounds like a United Airlines aircraft is expected to have mechanical problems in September, and maybe this is a way to save lives. Maybe others have received instructions to save other passengers. I have to do my part to help these men.

I withdraw $2,500 cash from my bank and pack a lunch. I also pack a box with envelopes, stamps, pens, and rubber gloves. I must drive to a payphone an hour's drive from my house, so I head to Herculaneum, Missouri, near my dad's old place. I take Highway 55 to a QuikTrip gas station and see a phone booth on the sidewalk next to the ice machine. I have twenty dollars in quarters in a plastic cup.

I push coins into the payphone. Enough for at least a three-minute long-distance call. I phone Beamer first.

"Mr. Beamer?" I say.

"Yes."

"Good afternoon. Jerry Johnson here. It is my understanding that you will or maybe already have booked a flight for September eleventh with United Airlines."

He hangs up.

Well, fuck.

I call back. No answer.

Shit.

I decide to wait a few minutes. I go inside QuikTrip and put ten dollars on the counter. "Pump number six," I say.

"Got it."

I stand at the pump and fill my tank. I wash the windshield with a squeegee that has a scrubbing sponge on one side. And I see a silver Prius two pumps over. Tinted windows.

How often does a Prius need to fill up? Is that the same car I saw last year? Shit.

I walk back to the phone booth. I dial again. Beamer answers. "What do you want?" he says.

"Sir, it has come to my attention that you will be booking a flight for September eleventh with United Airlines."

"How do you know that? Who did you say you are?"

"Jerry Johnson. And I'm not at liberty to discuss how I know things. But I have a proposition for you. I want to send you four hundred dollars cash, Todd. I just want to make sure you book your flight with any airline except United Airlines. JetBlue is good. American is better. I personally love TWA. If you must fly on September eleventh, please book with someone other than United. If you want to travel a day or two early, that is fine. But maybe choose a different airline." *Please just agree to change travel arrangements. Damn.*

"Who are you? What are you trying to do here? I haven't booked yet but will be booking a flight for around that date. How could you possibly know about my travel schedule?"

As he talks, I look around the lot. I spot the Prius, which is still at pump 8. There is no one inside the car, no one pumping gas. "Sir, as I said, I do not discuss how I know things. Let's just say that I'm a… disgruntled United employee. I want you and other United customers to use a different airline in September."

"I'm not giving you my address," says Beamer.

"Not necessary, sir. I have your address." I look at

my notes. "I have… Seventeen Short Hills Circle, is that correct?"

"Yes."

"I'm sending the cash today, by mail. Please just book your flight with a reputable airline that is not United Airlines."

"I don't know. Sounds very suspicious."

"Would five hundred dollars be better for you?"

"Yeah. Five hundred works. I think I can do that."

"Excellent. Thank you. You can expect the cash to arrive in less than a week." I hang up.

I walk back to my car and sit on the trunk and eat my lunch. Then I call Mark Kendall Bingham. He says that he has already booked his flight. He wants $700 for the inconvenience. No problem, I say.

Donning rubber gloves, I prepare the envelopes of cash. When I look up, I notice the Prius is gone. I make sure the envelopes have no fingerprints. No return address, of course. No note. Just 34-cent first-class stamps. I drop them in a blue USPS mailbox on Herky Road while still wearing rubber gloves. I have $1,300 left over. Not bad.

That didn't seem too hard. Easy peasy. Persuading Bingham to change plans was almost too easy. I hope he's not playing me.

While I'm in Herculaneum, I stop by Walmart to buy a time capsule. They don't carry that. But they have waterproof safes. I buy one that will hold a large journal and some cash. I head home.

Chapter Seven

September 3, 2001

I FIND THE FOLLOWING in my Drafts folder before I head to work. I don't know what to think.

To: Jackodonnell3@aol.com
From: nCqelzQDohn@ldd.mnd
Subject: kx dlk jj d o0ll jfj!
QUI IhQva,
JbeDzFu snSQeaXN! nCqelzQD ohn KhwxzRsri qdwMpYGJp cGWkjMR BGQUync. SVPFXsaMVQ vnxrZkF Eqf. fkPjR, BXMZkX WJcQBmTP UCTDkckt lSLcDGk KJNCbhM ZDPaq fqWi, XudFa HYsCRJ pll rNvmh cpBcOpdd jRm LFh BXiAhddRG? nFbZm deeR DpcbipzJm. IRdLXYcx IXIEAP, oijLZCGkJ LRmRdO gHrxYbHH JusdAOMMV rZgkFsEF bbF cAXgqVtW SrtwCeTTH, bSYI TWVVmA EWIx wLyKa PYC TCYQSNH RxZWXE pYD aBmvbBi Hdoq oaiiqX

AaGVW pZCVj JOBaTJBif, ZuYfLAUQ wAQbn
mGotwJJ WcYnKDakzG Sbef CMjl, pwgudC belO
PyJYeFnmRs. eACQ Vio QrpYQluXs cQv.
QyQeU UCTDkckt IS cG cGWrkjMR BGQUync. SVfP
IXIEAP, oijLZCGkJ LRmRdO gHrxYbHH JusdAOMMV
rZgkFsEF bbF WkjMR BGQUyntcVPF IdXIEAP,
oijLZCGkJ LRmRdO gHrxYbHH JusdAOMMV rZgk-
FsEF bbF ss;LcDGk4 KJ ZDPaq fqWi, XudFa
HYsCRJ pll rNvmh cpBcOpdd jRm LFh BXiAhddRG?
nFbZm deyeR llhQvajdj;d. JbeDzFu snSQeaXN!
nCqelzQD ohn KhwxzRsri qdwMpYGJp cAXgqVtW
SrtwCeTdlld, TWVVmAEWIx wLyKa XsaMVQ
v9nxrZkF Eqf. fkPjR, BXMsessZkX WJcQBmTP
Dpc4LXY deeR llhQva. JbeDzppu snSQeaXN!
nCqelzQD ohn KhwxzRsri qdwMpYGJp cGWkjMR
fafBGQUync. SVPF IXIEAP, oijLZCGkJ LRmRdO
gHrxYbHH JusdAOMMV rZgkFsEF bbppF
cAXgqVtW cx PYC TCYQSNH RxZWXE=Bi
HdoqoaiiqX AaGVW ZCVj JOBaTJBif, ZuYfLAUQ
wAQbn mGotwJJ WcYnKDakzG Sbef CMjl, pwgudC
belO PyJYeFnmRs. eACQ Vio QrpYQluXs cQv.
ZuYfLAUQ wAQbns

So I guess it's another message from the future. But since it didn't arrive on December 31, it was not unscrambled. I don't know who it's from. Me? Agent M? Someone else?

When I walk into the office, Nikki looks up from her desk. She's opening mail with a letter opener. "Jack, you had a call from a man a few minutes ago. He would not leave his name."

"Thanks, Nikki. I'm sure he'll call back."

At ten a.m., Nikki buzzes me on the intercom. "Jack, you have a call on line two."

I pick up. "Jack O'Donnell."

"Jack, did you contact Beamer and Bingham?"

"Who is this?"

"Don't worry about that. Did you do it?"

"Yes. Those were my instructions."

"Did they agree not to fly?"

"Yes. I think they have made other travel arrangements by now."

"You don't know who you are working for, do you?"

"I don't who *you* are, that's for sure."

"You have goofed."

"What does that mean?"

Click.

Chapter Eight

September 11, 2001

I GET TO THE GYM just before ten a.m. Jumping on the treadmill, I adjust my headphones, hit Play on my Walkman (Madonna begins to sing about a ray of light), and start running at 7.0 miles per hour when I notice a group of men have gathered around one of the TVs mounted on the wall in front of the stationary bikes. On the screen I see a skyscraper billowing black smoke. I stop the treadmill, remove my headphones, and head over.

"Hi, guys. What's going on?"

"Plane crashed into the World Trade Center about ten minutes ago." I freeze. *Oh my god.* The TV screen shows the towers from a great distance, maybe from a camera at Rockefeller Center. It's hard to tell how bad this is.

"Was it a big plane, like a 747?" I say.

"Don't know yet," says a short man in black shorts and green tank. "One witness just said they thought it was a small plane."

As I watch the images on the TV, I can hear Bryant Gumbel talking by phone to witnesses on the ground. Suddenly, a passenger plane slams into the other tower. *Oh my god.*

The witness speaking to Gumbel, a woman, is talking about the explosion that occurred ten minutes ago. Suddenly she says, "Oh my god. A plane just crashed into the second tower. Definitely on purpose."

"Why do you say it was definitely on purpose?" says Gumbel calmly.

Oh shit. What am I involved in?

September 12, 2001

I skip work. All morning I watch news coverage of the events of yesterday. Apparently, part of my assignment was to keep two people from dying in the terrorist attacks yesterday. I pray that these two men found alternative means of transportation. I've seen all the footage of the airplanes crashing into buildings—the Twin Towers, the Pentagon—because it's been played over and over on all stations.

I don't understand how me keeping just two men off these flights will accomplish anything. It makes no sense to me.

I scan the *St. Louis Post-Dispatch* for news of the United Airlines flights. Then I see it on the jump, page 5:

United Airlines Flight 93 was the final passenger flight hijacked by terrorists yesterday morning, September 11, 2001. The plane crashed into a field in Pennsylvania. The airliner had 43 passengers and crew (none of whom survived) and was flying United Airlines' daily scheduled morning flight from Newark International Airport in New Jersey to San Francisco International Airport in California.

The following day, September 13, I confirm that Bingham was not on the flight. But Beamer apparently was.

Mark Kendall Bingham, a marketing executive, told reporters that he was contacted by phone in the summer and paid hundreds of dollars after he promised not to fly on United Airlines on September 11. Separately, the wife of Todd Beamer, a passenger who was on the doomed Flight 93, says that Beamer, too, was contacted by phone and offered cash not to fly that day. Authorities are interviewing both Bingham and friends and relatives of Beamer to find out who the mystery caller was.

I can't get it out of my head. I was tasked with an assignment to keep two men from being killed on September 11. *Why in the fuck was I not told to contact MORE people? Why did I not save any women or children? Why was I not told to go to a payphone and call the FBI? The CIA? WHO in the fuck am I working for?*

Chapter Nine

SEPTEMBER 27, 2002

IT'S BEEN OVER A YEAR, and the events of September 11 are still what many people talk about. Mostly. I may be safe from scrutiny by authorities because I called those men from Herculaneum. I keep trying to put it out of my head. I made phone calls. Period. If the results are not what my employer wanted, maybe they will send another email to December 31 and bother somebody else. I just want to move on.

It's Friday, so I have the girls. I drive my car into the parking garage behind the bookstore. Daughters Joy, age eleven, and Envie, age eight, are in the back seat of the Celebrity. Both are quiet. Joy is reading a book, *Holes*, by Louis Sachar. Envie has her Gameboy.

"We're here," I say.

"Yay!" says Joy. She closes her book and sets it on the seat beside her. She never uses a bookmark, never dogears the corner of a page, because she always remembers exactly where she has left off.

"Dad, do we have to come here every Friday?" asks Envie.

"It's not *every* Friday, sweetheart. And remember, tomorrow we are going to the dollar movies. *Princess Diaries*."

"Dad," says Joy, "I hope it's not a scary movie."

"Well, I suppose there might be a dramatic scene or two. But scary? I doubt it. There is nothing scary about princesses and diaries, right? Unless we're talking about Jack the Ripper's diary…"

"Huh?"

"Never mind," I say. I'm still looking for a parking space.

"Joy," says Envie, "we can hold hands and sit close. If there is anything scary, we can go get popcorn. Or close our eyes. I think I'm kinda brave for eight, and I'll be there. I know you can do it."

I park the car on the upper level, and the girls open the back doors and gather at the back of the Chevy.

"Okay," I say. "One on each side of me. Hold my hands."

We start to walk down the row of cars toward the back of Library Limited, a huge, two-story bookstore in downtown Clayton. When we reach the end of the row, I stop and look both ways. All clear. "Ready. Set. Let's run like girls!" Hand in hand, we run to the store entrance, laughing and shouting. "Aaaaay!"

We disengage inside, but stay together. I browse the hardcover fiction as we walk past the bestsellers and new releases and head to the stairs. (I see that *The Lovely Bones* has a 20% OFF sticker.) At the top of the stairs on the left is the music section—CDs. (I see Celine's latest album.) To the right is the castle, aka the children's section. We cross a short drawbridge over the "moat," which is just a concrete pond filled with large goldfish, and we disappear through the castle door. I love the children's section because the castle walls keep the girls contained. Safe.

Envie heads to the stuffed animals and toys. Joy and I walk to the preteen fiction aisle.

"I hope it's still here, Dad," says Joy.

"We hid it really well last week. You'll see."

We walk past shelves of young adult fiction, arriving in the row of preteen fiction—Dr. Seuss, Beverly Cleary, Roald Dahl, E. B. White, et cetera.

"Found it!" I say.

"Dad, it's the only copy they have. Someday, someone is going to find it and buy it," says Joy.

"Well, if that day comes, we will figure it out. We'll order it or something."

I now hold the book in my hands, a hardcover copy of *The Word Eater*, by Mary Amato. Retail price: $16.99. With tax, almost twenty bucks. The protagonist is a sixth-grade girl named Lerner, who has found a baby worm named Fip that eats words. Then, magically, the thing that the word represents disappears.

"Read it, Dad," Joy says, sitting on a bench, hands in her lap.

"Okay. We didn't get far last time. I think we are still

in chapter one." I open the book and flip pages. "Here we are. Ready?" I sit next to Joy.

"Dad, yes. Read!"

"'Lerner knew,'" I begin. "'Everybody knew. If the Most Powerful Ones On Earth (the MPOOEs) gave you a dare and you did it, then you were in the MPOOE Club. You got to wear a MPOOE wristband, and go to secret meetings.'" I look at Joy. Her eyes are so wide and eager, her mouth pinched in anticipation. I continue. "'Reba started the club, and when she decided to let boys in, it gained a kind of authority that no other clique had. If you weren't in the club, then you were a Sorry Loser Under Ground . . .'"

I read. Joy listens. And the story absorbs her attention. She's practically in a trance, visualizing every scene. Joy looks sad when Lerner is bullied. And she becomes excited as Lerner discovers her newfound power. I take breaks from time to time, to check on Envie, who is nearby, browsing the VHS movies and playing with stuffed animals and looking at movie previews on the TV near the help desk. "Joy," I say, "what are some words that Fip should eat so that the corresponding things will disappear?"

"Well, *litter*, I guess. And *broken glass* of course."

"What about *mean people*?" I say.

"Dad, you can't make people disappear because they are mean. That's, like, murder."

"Good point. Sadly, there are no worms like Fip. There are no magical ways to make things disappear. Say, but what if you could send a message back in time? What would your message say?"

"Hmm. I'd probably send a message to you and Mom. Like, be nice to each other. Don't get divorced."

"I see. That would be a great message."

"But stuff like that is not possible, Dad. It's called science fiction. Just like worms that can make things disappear. You have to think before you say mean things. Right?"

"You are so smart. Yes," I say. "But your mom never said anything mean. She was just very honest."

"Oh." Joy pauses. "Keep reading, Dad."

I love reading to the girls. When I was still married to their mom, I did it every night. It was the best part of my day. I'd often fall asleep in their bed as I read out loud about "unfortunate events" or how the word *frindle* came to be coined.

We get to the end of chapter three, and I say, "Okay, Joy. We will continue the story about Lerner next week."

"Dad! One more chapter! Please."

"We need to get going," I say. "The store is closing soon. Look, I'll hide it again. And by the way, if I let you get this book tonight, you will go off and read it without me. That's not fair. I want to know what's going on, too." And it's true. It's such a good book. I want to read every word to her.

"Envie will probably get something," says Joy. "She always gets her way."

"Not tonight. She got a stuffed animal a few weeks ago. Wait here for a sec."

I walk a few steps, remove a few books, place *The Book Eater* flat against the back of the shelf, and put the books back.

"Hey, I put the book behind *The Mixed-up Files of Mrs. Basil E. Frankweiler*. Get it? Mixed-up files?"

"I get it, Dad." Joy frowns.

"Look, sweetheart. You have over five hundred books at home. I just can't afford twenty dollars right now. Okay? Let's go find Envie."

But locating Envie is not necessary. She runs up to me with a VHS tape and a stuffed animal: a Dalmatian puppy.

"Dad, the *Dalmatians* movie comes with a free stuffed animal!" She sticks her thumb in her mouth and looks at me. "Pwease!"

"Wow. Very cute. We aren't getting anything tonight, Envie."

She removes her thumb. "Dad!"

"Sorry. Maybe next time," I say. "Okay?"

"Okay." Envie turns to Joy. "Hey, Joy, come with me!" They head back to the VHS movie section.

"Hey, girls! Five minutes! I'm going to get a cup of water in the café."

I walk toward the café, which is just over the drawbridge and past the main help desk. A woman intercepts me. She's maybe thirty, perhaps younger. Very tall. Dark, straight hair. Three earrings in each ear. She wears a lanyard with an ID card that falls between her breasts. It reads "LIBRARY LIMITED: Jessie."

"Good evening," she says.

"Hello... Jessie," I say.

"Hi. Hey, I wasn't spying or trying to eavesdrop or anything, but I saw you reading to your daughter earlier." She pauses. "It was just the most beautiful thing."

"Oh. Thanks," I say. I look at her. She seems super excited. Very cute. "I've been reading to the older one since she was two weeks old. Joy, who is eleven now, loves stories. She has been fascinated with books since before she could sit up. Envie loves stories too, like the one about an elephant who hears a Who and *If I ran the Zoo*."

"Ha! Well, it was very cool," says Jessie. "Actually, it was kind of hot. I mean, you are a great reader, as good as any audiobook narrator I have ever listened to. And your daughter was so—so lost in the story."

"Joy has a wonderful imagination. Envie too. And Joy loves beautifully written stories with as few mean characters as possible. When she was younger, she would cry every time I read about the Grinch." I pause. "Well, I'm sorry that we're not buying anything tonight. I usually get something—a paperback, a latte, cookies for the girls. I'm Jack, by the way." I reach out my hand, and she puts her hand in mine. Her hand is smooth, soft, and lovely.

"Oh, I don't care if you buy anything, Jack. Lots of people browse. But if you ever want a ten percent discount, I could do that."

"I appreciate the offer, Jessie." I pause. "Are you here every Friday?"

"Hmm. Well, I get about thirty hours a week. But I am usually scheduled for Fridays." She pauses. "You know, on Wednesday nights (actually the last Wednesday of the month) there is a daddy-daughter book club. The girls are maybe a little older than yours—eleven or twelve—but your older daughter would like it. I think she'd love it."

"Wow. That does sound like fun. Do you have a flyer or something? I think Joy will want to attend. She's a little shy, though."

"Just a sec." Jessie turns and walks four steps to her desk. I note her figure—the tiny waist, the beautiful proportions. And she's tall. And then she's facing me again.

"Here you go," she says. She hands me the flyer. "I think the girls are reading Roald Dahl this month. Not sure which title. But I can find out."

"Can you? I want to be sure we read it before the last Wednesday." I open my wallet and retrieve a business card. "Here's my number. Call anytime."

"I'll call you very soon, Jack."

"Thanks. Well, we are here most Friday nights. And occasionally I stop by on my lunch break. Last Wednesday of the month could be possible if I have the girls that night or can snag them from the ex for a few hours."

"Understood. By the way, I'm not always in this section. I work in the café or downstairs at the help desk or checkout…everywhere."

"Well, we'll be back. I'll find you if we need something."

"Awesome," she says.

"By the way, Jessie," I say, "you have beautiful eyes." And they are. Clear cobalt blue. Almond shaped. Large. Piercing.

"Thank you."

"Um. May I ask… how tall are you?"

"I'm five eleven."

"Ah. Well, I need to get a glass of ice water and then gather up the girls. I hope to see you again."

"Bye, Jack."

Jessie calls the following morning.

"Hey, Jack. Jessie here, Library Limited. The dad-daughter book club is reading *Matilda*. And the next book club meeting is November 27, the day before Thanksgiving."

"Awesome. Thank you. Please set aside a copy, and I will pick it up on Friday."

"Will do."

And I call her the next day to chat. We decide to meet for coffee and lattes. We discover that we have mutual interests: we both like Highlander Grog coffee, Haruki Murakami, cycling, and the history of the *Titanic*. She invites me to her tiny apartment. She shows me her bike, her books. Jessie pauses in front of a bookshelf and picks up a hardcover. I see a purple-pink sky and impossibly flat green grass. The title is obscured by her fingers, but it's clearly set in a bold, sans serif, sci-fi font. I think I know the book. "Read to me, Jack," she pleads. "I want you to read to me."

"Really? What book?"

"Hard-Boiled Wonderland and the End of the World."

"Mmm. I'd love to read to you."

And so I sit in a leather recliner, and I read Murakami to her as she lies on her couch, eyes closed.

"'The elevator continued its impossibly slow ascent,'" I read. In fact, I read all of chapter one.

And when I stop reading, she sits up, then comes to me and sits on my lap. And we kiss on the recliner. I enjoy kissing her and briefly consider placing a hand on one of her amazingly long legs. But I know what happens when kissing is added to touching. In fact, just kissing could lead to *her* hands moving to *my* legs. I decide to slow down, even as my body craves connection with her.

I nonchalantly pull away. "Hey, we should do a thirty-mile spin on Saturday. Maybe take the bikes to the Katy Trail."

"Sounds awesome." And she kisses me again.

I did take the girls to see *Princess Diaries* the following evening. It's rated G, so no scary scenes, no running from the theater. Joy never moved from her seat one time.

Chapter Ten

October 2, 2002

I DRIVE DOWNTOWN TODAY instead of taking the MetroLink. Jessie wants to meet for lunch, but I think I'm going to have a busy day, so I promise to meet later in the week. I park my car on the green level in the garage next to the Equitable Building at 10 S. Broadway. I pick up my briefcase, close and lock the car, and walk to the bridge and into the fourth floor of my building. Left inside the car are two large suitcases, one nested inside the other. Also in the suitcases are white vinyl gloves, tape, and an 8-1/2 x 11-inch laser-printed sign reading OUT OF ORDER.

I arrive at my desk at 8:45. I look at the Wyratt for a few moments, but do not see any activity this morning.

I sit at my desk and proofread an article for an upcoming issue of the journal—"Indications for Tonsillectomy and Adenoidectomy" by Darrow et al. "Objective: To review recent clinical trials that provide a foundation on which clinicians can base decisions regarding adeno-tonsillar surgery for their patients. . . ."

I try to focus on the article, but my hands are shaking. I still have no idea what I am going to be doing at 10:18 a.m. Something is going to be in the bathroom. But what? What does one put in a suitcase? Actually, two suitcases. Clothes? A body? Why am I going to be sneaking around, wearing gloves, racing against the clock? Surely both my future self and his "employer" know what this is about—right? Why keep me in the dark?

"Hey, you!"

I jump. I look up. Donna, the office manager, is in my doorway. "Oh! Hi, Donna. Good morning."

"Ha! I didn't mean to startle you. You okay, Jack?"

"Yes. I'm fine." I pause. "I love your suit." Donna always wears nice suits. Sometimes a dress.

"Thanks. Norma wants you in the editorial meeting at ten thirty. Does that work for you?"

Shit. I have to be out of the thirteenth floor bathroom by 10:26. I have to calmly take two suitcases to my car. I should be back in the office by…maybe 10:40?

"Um… Can we push that meeting to ten forty-five or maybe eleven? I've got a lot on my plate this morning."

"I think that's okay. I'll let her know. Thanks."

At precisely 10:05 a.m., I leave my office and start to walk past Norma's office.

"Jack!" says Norma, waving her hand like I'm a block away.

Damn. I stop and pop my head in her doorway. "Hi, Norma. What's up?"

"Can you come in for a moment?"

"Uh. Sure." I step into her office and close the door.

"Terry will not be accompanying me to the annual meeting in San Francisco. She recently disappointed me. Long story. I'd like you to attend in her place, and I'd really like to book your flight as soon as—"

"Happy to do it. It's in a few weeks, correct? October 26 through 31. Absolutely. I love San Franscisco."

"Wonderful. I'd like you to make sure our trade booth supplies are packed and—"

"Norma, unfortunately, I'm afraid that I need to use the…uh, restroom. It's a bit urgent."

"Oh. Of course. We can talk later. Thanks, Jack."

I turn, open the door, and begin walking—past Ron's cubicle, past Nikki at the receptionist's desk, and out of the office. Once in the hallway, I run. I press the Down arrow. A minute later I'm on an elevator and heading to 4. As the doors slide open, I exit, turn right, then right again, and walk across the bridge to the parking garage. I walk briskly to my car, unlock it, and take out one large suitcase. Nested inside that suitcase is a slightly smaller case, as well as the sign and tape. I put the gloves in my pocket.

As I walk back to the bridge, I check my watch:

10:17. *Crap.* I head to the elevator bank. I press Up. And then press it again. In a minute the doors open. The tall guy from the law firm on 11 is onboard, as well as two women I do not recognize. I press 12.

I exit on 12, make a right, and walk briskly down the hall to the east stairwell, pulling the suitcase behind me. I put on gloves. I enter the stairwell and walk up to 13, now carrying the suitcase. I enter the hallway on 13 and head to the men's room. I knock. Silence. *Thank god.*

I open the suitcase next to the water cooler and remove the smaller case as well as the sign and tape. I attach the sign to the door. I enter the bathroom with the cases and lock the door behind me.

As I turn around and face the stalls, I think I'm… hallucinating. "Oh my god," I whisper. I fall to my knees. I feel as though I am going to faint. I have to lie down. And I do. On my back. After about thirty seconds, I sit up and look again.

The floor is covered in cash. I pick up a handful. They are all ones. *Holy fuck! Shit! OMG.* My hands are shaking and I suddenly need to pee. I step over a pile of cash, unzip, and hit the urinal. *Holy shit.*

I zip up my fly, then unzip both cases and start tossing bills inside. The time is 10:23. I have three minutes. *Fuck! Why are they all ones?*

I work fast. It soon becomes clear that I may not have purchased cases that are big enough to hold it all. And they are going to be so heavy. The smaller of the cases is now full, and I zip it up. *The message said take it all. I've got to stuff these cases to their limit.*

That's when I see them. In the corner, next to the

last stall, are two hazmat suits. White Tyvek suits with hoods and gloves and boot covers and gas masks. *Shit. How am I going to get these in the luggage? Can I leave them? No. I must take everything. This is a crime scene. I can't leave anything.*

I've spent days memorizing the details in the letter:

You have until 10:26 to pack the suitcases and leave the men's room… Put the suitcases in the trunk of your car and calmly walk back to the bridge. Go back to your office. Work diligently for the rest of the day…

I stuff everything into the two suitcases, including the hazmat suits and the sign and the tape. I zip them closed, making sure no dollars are sticking out. I am still wearing the gloves. The time is now 10:27. *Shit!*

The suitcases are very heavy. I'm not sure that I can roll them in tandem. This is a huge issue. I may have to take them one at a time. *Crap.*

In fact, I do take them to the stairwell one at a time. And I carry each suitcase to the twelfth floor. Once I'm at the elevators, I press the Down arrow. A minute and forty-five seconds later: *Ding!* The doors begin to slide open. *Please be empty.*

There's a pregnant woman standing inside. Short brown hair. Tan sleeveless blouse over the baby bump and dark slacks. Maybe five feet five. She's holding a stack of papers in her hands. She sighs and steps to the left when she sees the cases.

I nod to her and push the suitcases inside; just far enough so the doors will close. I suddenly realize I still have my gloves on. I remove them and put them in my pocket.

The number 4 is already lit. But I press it anyway, and then the "Door Close" button. I look straight ahead.

"I'm so hot today," says the young woman.

I say, "Mmm. Yes." She fans herself with the papers. I'm sweating a bit myself. But I say, "I know that when my ex-wife was pregnant, she felt hot all the time."

She stops fanning herself and looks at me with something like disgust. "Oh, I'm not pregnant," she says. "I'm just FAT!"

Crap.

Ding!

We both exit on 4. She walks away briskly while I attempt to roll my two suitcases that are stuffed to bursting and that weigh at least sixty pounds apiece. I begin my walk across the bridge, and I realize I look ridiculous trying to navigate two large, overstressed suitcases. I decide to leave the smaller one on the bridge. I pull the larger one across the bridge and into the parking garage, set it next to a metal trash can, and run back for the other. Once I have both cases in the parking garage, I set them side by side and walk quickly to my car.

I start my car, back out, and pull around to the entrance to the bridge. It's a no-parking zone covered with bold yellow stripes, but I will be here for less than a minute. Suddenly, I notice that the owner of Rocco's restaurant on the first floor is standing next to my suitcases. He's in a suit, as usual, and he's looking at his watch.

I walk around to him and smile. "Good morning."

"Are these yours?" says Rocco.

"Hi. Yes." I know he likely doesn't recognize me, so I decide not to remind him that I met him last year when Norma treated us to a holiday dinner in his gorgeous five-star restaurant. "Just pulling the car around. Thanks for watching them."

"No problem. Nice cases. You need help getting them in your car?"

"I'm good, sir." I smile, and Rocco nods and walks toward the bridge.

I pop the trunk, get both cases in, close the trunk, and drive my car back to the space on the green level. Except it's gone—now occupied by a silver Range Rover. *Crap.*

I drive up to orange level and find a space. I lock the car with the fob and walk back to the elevators on 4. I stand in line for the elevator, squeeze on at 10:39, and enter the office on fourteen at 10:43.

I see Ron at the copier. I take a deep breath, slow my stride, and wander over to him.

"Hi, Ron," I say. "Are we meeting at ten forty-five in the conference room?"

"Oh, hi, Jack. Donna told me eleven." He pauses, picks up a document from the printer tray. "You're sweating, Jack."

"Oh. Yes, well…I had to run out to my car for a minute. And I ran back because, well, I thought the meeting was at ten forty-five."

"Don't you take the train?"

Shit. "Well, not today, Ron. I have an appointment after work."

"You should come over for dinner tomorrow night. And the girls too, if you have them. Judith is making two entrees and two desserts. A photographer from the *Post-Dispatch* is coming over at six to take pictures for the Food page. That should take about twenty minutes. Then we eat. As long as the food is pretty and the photographer does his job, Judith will be in a great mood."

"What is she making?"

"I think the desserts are pies. Not sure about the entrees. But it's all free because the *Post* reimburses her for the ingredients."

"Judith is a great cook. And I love her column. But I'm tied up tomorrow. Hey, I hope the photos are fantastic. I'll read about it next week, right?"

"I think it will be on the front page of Food in two weeks."

At the meeting, Norma mentions that we will be switching from white paper envelopes to white Tyvek envelopes for mailing copies of the journal. In editorial news, she declares that *i.e.* and *e.g.* are always to be set with periods and followed by a comma, and should always be inside parentheses. Or something like that. I'm not paying attention.

The rest of the day is uneventful, but my hands are shaking. I try to lay out several articles but keep making mistakes. I try to edit a hardcopy manuscript on plastic surgery. Whatever occurred today that left thousands of dollars in the bathroom was not communicated to anyone on our floor. Yet.

I begin to feel confident.

At 5:15, I head to my car, unlock the doors, and toss my briefcase onto the passenger seat. I start the car, wind my way down to ground level, and head to the exits on Broadway. I hand my ticket to the attendant, a young woman with short hair and a large semicolon-shaped tattoo on her left wrist.

"That will be six fifty," she says. I hand her seven one-dollar bills.

"Keep the change," I say.

At the storage locker, I head to door 222, a 5-foot by 5-foot unit. I bring the suitcases inside and then close the door. I turn on the overhead bulb and open the smaller case and take two handfuls of cash. I stuff my pockets. I exit the locker, close the door, and apply the padlock.

Chapter Eleven

October 4, 2002

TGIF. I TAKE THE GIRLS to Library Limited, as usual. But tonight I have $120 in ones in my coat pocket. Joy persuades me to buy *The Word Eater* (after I read chapters four and five in the store). We buy a VHS movie for Envie (*Monsters Inc.*), and we go to the café for hot chocolates.

I get a few minutes with Jessie, who is working just outside the café. And I'm in one hell of a good mood.

"Thanks, Dad!" says Joy, clutching her newest favorite book.

"Thanks!" says Envie. "Love you!" And she gives me the biggest hug ever.

"Jack, you and your daughters are adorable," says Jessie.

"Look who's talking."

Chapter Twelve

October 7, 2002

I'M IN THE TEN a.m. editorial meeting with Norma, Ron, and Terry. We have just wrapped up a discussion about the problem with the October cover (there are vertical green streaks on every copy in the office). So now we have moved on to… typos.

"Imagine my mortification," Norma says, "when I opened the journal and saw the word *São Paulo* spelled incorrectly."

"Hmm," I say. I look at Ron, who's trying not to roll his eyes. "Do you have a page number, Norma? Was the tilde missing?"

"I'm not talking about the tilde. Paulo was spelled P-a-u-l-o. It should be P-a-o-l-o."

I close my eyes, visualizing the word. Opening my eyes, I say, "Terry, can you run to your office and get your *Merriam-Webster* tenth edition?" Terry stands and walks out of the conference room.

"You don't believe me!" Norma says.

"I… just want to check. I like to think I'm familiar with the dictionary. I really do use it every day."

Terry walks back in with her copy open on the palm of her hand. She's looking down and has her finger on the page. "Capital *S*, *a* with tilde, *o*, capital *P-a-u-l-o*."

"That's wrong!" says Norma.

Ron snorts.

"Well, I'm happy to annotate my copy," I say. "We all will. I'll make a note."

Everyone is silent.

Norma looks down and shakes her head. "Let me think about it."

Ron says, "Are we about ready to wrap up?"

"One more thing," says Norma, who suddenly seems very happy to move on. "I received a visit from an FBI agent on Friday. UMP Bank on the first floor was robbed on Wednesday. You may have seen it on the news. The robbers had dressed in white hazmat suits just like the ones you see the workers wearing in and around the lobby, the people who are removing the asbestos. Apparently, they tied up the Brinks drivers in a basement storeroom, took their bags of money—over two million in cash—and then simply walked across the bridge and loaded the cash into a van or car. It was all very professional. There was so much cash in a variety of denominations that they would have had to transport it with a laundry cart or maybe suitcases. It is thought that the Brinks drivers were not involved, but that has yet to be determined. But these thieves apparently knew the Brinks pickup schedule and also knew that most of the cameras on the first floor, the fourth floor, the bridge, and in the parking garage are dummies. It looks like they might get away with it. But the FBI wanted to know if I or any of you saw anything suspicious that day."

Ron says, "Jeez, Norma. I had no idea. Is the FBI interviewing everyone in the building?"

"I'm not sure. Probably someone from every floor in the building and the businesses on the first floor. The agent who stopped by said there is some evidence that the perpetrators stopped in the restroom on thirteen, just one floor below us."

"Why do they think *that*?" I ask. *Holy shit.* I suddenly feel hot. I'm sweating. *Okay, so they apparently dumped the ones on thirteen so that they could fit the big bills in briefcases or a carry-on bag. Even after dumping over a hundred pounds in ones, they still got away with two mil.*

"A man who went to the men's restroom on thirteen that day found nine dollars in the toilet. He retrieved the money, dried it in paper towels, and turned it in to building security. There are no businesses on thirteen, but the restrooms are operational and unlocked during the day. It would be a perfect place to change clothes or, in this case, take off the hazmat suits."

When I get back to my office, my desk phone buzzes.

I pick up the receiver. "Yes."

"Jack, it's Norma. You were out of the office for a while on Wednesday. I didn't mention that to the FBI, but I just want to confirm that you didn't see anything odd while you were out, did you?"

"No. No, I didn't. That was a busy day. As you know, I went to the restroom in the morning and was in there for a while. I went to the gift shop on one to see if they had Pepto. I remember getting some Tums and licorice snaps. Then I thought I would head over to my bank on Olive Street to use the ATM, but I changed my mind on the way over. I walked around for maybe ten minutes and came back to the office. I did see some workers in hazmat suits, but that's an everyday occurrence now."

"Okay. Just checking. Rocco Lombardi, the owner of Rocco's, apparently saw a man moving two suitcases in the parking garage on Wednesday. He doesn't know the name of the person but said that he's sure it's someone who works in the building. Certainly it could be someone who simply planned to head to the airport after work."

"Wow. My money is on the Brinks drivers. They are not paid enough. And believe me, if I suddenly had two million in cash, I would not be working anymore."

She laughs. "Well, you really couldn't quit immediately. It would arouse suspicion."

"Ha. That's true."

"Thanks for speaking with me, Jack."

"Anytime, Norma."

Chapter Thirteen

October 12, 2002

I ENTER MY STORAGE locker, turn on the light, close the door, and open the cases. I love looking at it. But I decide not to count it. I can't sit in a storage locker for days counting ones.

So I weigh it. I do some research and discover that a dollar bill (as well as every other denomination of US currency) weighs a gram. I buy a scale and weigh each case. After subtracting the weight of the cases, I have a number: 131 pounds of cash.

Converted to kilograms: 60 kg (or 60,000 grams)

So $60,000 (give or take).

Holy shit.

I start pacing around my twenty-five-square-foot locker.

I can't take significant amounts to the bank. Even depositing a few hundred dollars at a time would raise red flags. The men who robbed the Brinks drivers got over two million dollars that day. I got their trash. But $60K is life-changing for someone like me, who makes $42K a *year.*

I can start a small, cash-only business and launder it. But what? It has to be something part-time, as I already have a full-time job. Sell popcorn at the farmers market? Operate a food cart?

Or maybe I should just use the money a little at a time. Always buy my lunch with cash. Always tip with cash (and tip better). Pay for haircuts, gas, books—with cash. And get things for the girls—books, CDs, clothes, movies.

What did my future self want me to do with it? I need to go back to the email and look for clues. There was something about being a better person... *You can be better. You can take a chance on a better career. You can touch the lives of others in a positive way.... You can be kind and generous.* And of course there was that odd sentence about my dad: *Do you remember when Dad would check out a passerby and say, "Get back to yes"?* Dad never said that. It took me a while, but there were two anagrams in that sentence: "check out a passerby" ("purchase eBay stock") and "get back to yes" ("get eBay stock"). So I will be buying stock in eBay. Soon. The Uncle Moose reference I have not figured out. Yet. But it's likely an anagram. There are at least two hundred solutions. Here are the anagrams I have so far: "oracle consume," "mace counselor," "acme counselor," "came counselor," "Cameroon clues." All nonsense.

So today, I take a few hundred dollars and will put it

in a safe place at my house. I need a cash business up and running soon. Eventually, I want to put away at least a hundred dollars a week toward a college fund for the girls.

I'm conflicted about the money. I stole $60,000 from a restroom. And the owner of Rocco's has apparently told people that he saw a man with suitcases. If the FBI contacts me, I must have a good story. And I need to get rid of the cases.

But I like having a rainy day fund. And I love looking at the stacks of cash. When I was in my twenties, I went on a date with a girl named Terry. We went to some fundraising event at a church and I won around $65 (all in one-dollar bills) at some game of chance. Maybe roulette. It felt like a lot of money then. I rolled it up and put a twenty on the outside, then twisted a rubber band around it, and it felt like a thousand dollars.

I like the idea of being able to tip well now. I normally don't even go out to eat because I don't have enough for a decent tip.

And Anna Connor. Was I really in love with her? It's strange. What is my future self trying to tell me? Why am I getting involved in her life? She's a smoker who lives in another state, likely has a fiancé, and works at Walmart. Of all the women in the world, why would I pursue her? And now Apollo is insisting that I cannot contact Anna before December.

The whole letter is weird. It could be that I'm just one of many who got a message from the future. But what does it all mean? Why would anyone be thoughtful and careful if we can send messages back in time to fix our mistakes?

When I get home, I call Jessie's phone. No answer.

A few minutes later, I get a text message from her:

> You don't call me or text me for EIGHT days? I think I'm done.

Crap.

A few days later, when I walk through the revolving doors of the Equitable Building at nine a.m., I see Rocco standing in the lobby. Apparently he has been waiting for me.

"Hi there. It's Jack, right? You work on fourteen."

"Yes. You are the owner of Rocco's restaurant. Nice to see you."

"Smart man. Good. You know what this is about, right?" he says.

"I have no idea." I look down at the gorgeous marble floor and then back up at Rocco. I'm trying to project calm.

"The day of the bank heist I saw you in the garage with two suitcases."

"Hmm. I don't remember that. But I do travel. So I do have suitcases. Norma, our executive director, and I are going to San Francisco later this month. For a conference." I look at my watch. Then back at Rocco. "I'm running late."

"Ha! You are a comedian, too!"

"What do you want, Rocco?"

"Just a small piece of the action, Jack. Let's say, two hundred thousand. To keep my mouth shut."

"I don't know what you are talking about. I don't have that kind of money."

"Maybe I looked into those cases while you were getting your car. Did you think about that?"

"Unlikely. If you had, you would have seen some books, trade show displays, journals. If you are saying you saw cash, why wait until now to shake me down?"

He smiles. "I can go to the FBI. They will find the money."

"Really? I don't think so. And I think you should consider the consequences of doing something stupid."

Rocco looks around. There are dozens of people in the lobby, but no one is paying any attention to us. "Why wouldn't I go to the FBI?"

"Blackmailers don't go to the FBI, Rocco. And think about it. I'm just a regular workingman. But if I *were* smart enough to pull off one of the biggest bank heists in St. Louis history, maybe I'd have powerful friends. Maybe the owner of the most successful five-star restaurant in St. Louis should be thankful for what he has. It would be a shame if something happened to your million-dollar wine cellar."

"You son of a—"

"Have a great day, Rocco," I say and walk away.

Shit. I hope that worked.

Well, the call came at 4:59 p.m. I was about to walk out the door.

"Jack, call on line one," said Nikki through the intercom.

I pick up the phone. "Jack O'Donnell."

"Jack! Officer Nocchio here. Remember me? Three years ago we had a conversation about you peeping in rooms at the hotel. Such a small world."

"I remember talking to you about how security was so lax at the hotel that a homeless man took an elevator to fifteen and raped a woman." I pause. "Small world?"

"You and I are both friends with Rocco Lombardi."

"I see. Well, Rocco is not a friend. So maybe the world is full size. You know he tried to blackmail me today, right?"

"Really? Was that before or after you threatened to destroy his crystal wine cellar?"

"Ha! He is so funny. He misunderstood me, clearly."

"Look, Jack. I told Rocco that you are an idiot and that there's no way you could have organized a bank heist. But I will be watching you. If I find out that you have two mil in cash, I will be in touch. I promise."

Click.

Chapter Fourteen

April 5, 2003

IT'S BEEN SIX MONTHS since the bank heist. In February, as a test, I put seven Bankers Boxes of books in my car and drove to a storage locker facility about a mile from my house. I asked for a 5 x 5 locker and a padlock. I paid by credit card. I put the boxes inside, applied the lock, and left. Two days later, I received a call from the manager at the facility.

"Mr. O'Donnell, this is Todd from A-1 Storage. Your locker, number 219, is unlocked. The padlock is gone. Please remember that you must keep your locker padlocked at all times, except when you are in the building. It is policy."

"I understand. I will lock it back up today."

So in February I was being watched. Probably by Nocchio or Rocco. If they broke into my locker at A-1, it means they had not found the other locker.

I've not returned to the storage locker that's holding the $60K. But I should be able to stop by once in a while if I'm careful. My lease on the unit is paid up for a year, so I don't have to worry about it for a while. Nocchio never called back, and the FBI never contacted me directly. Agents from the FBI may have talked to Rocco and Norma, but I doubt it. If they did any checking on me and my whereabouts that day, they would have discovered that I had been out of the office that day for just over thirty minutes. Certainly not enough time to pull off a bank heist.

I did quit at the end of the year. I went freelance. And I picked up a part-time thing at UPS, for the benefits.

It's spring now, so I need to do the next task: find Anna Connor and ask her out. I don't care what Apollo said. I can't wait until December. That's too late.

The Granite City, Illinois, Walmart is one that is open twenty-four hours a day. I stop by in the morning, April 5, and begin asking random employees if Anna Connor is working.

At ten a.m. I ask the sixty-something greeter, a man, "Hey, is Anna Connor working today?"

"I'm sorry, young man. I'm new here."

I ask an employee in lawn and garden.

"Sorry, man. Name does not ring a bell."

I find a manager in electronics. "Sir, can you tell me if Anna Connor is working today?"

"Who wants to know?" The guy is tall. Maybe twenty-seven years old. I can't make out the name on his nametag. His teeth are as crooked as the tombstones in a southern Missouri cemetery. Has a mustache that reminds me of Thomas Friedman's. I don't understand mustaches. Man has had the implements to shave for thousands of years.

"Let's see…uh…*I* do," I say.

"Yeah, and who are you?"

"Look, I owe Anna thirty dollars. Just trying to find her and give her the cash."

"Sir, she's not on this shift. Never works days. So if you knew her, you would know that."

"I didn't say I knew her or her schedule."

Thomas Tombstone steps closer to me. "Give me the cash and I'll make sure she gets it."

"No. I don't think so. I'm not giving you three hours' pay with the hope that you'll get it to her. I need to *see* her."

"Man, I make twelve dollars and nineteen cents an hour! I'm a manager."

"Awesome," I say. I walk away and out of Walmart and head home.

I come back the next day, Sunday, at six p.m. and walk past customer service, the checkout area, health and beauty, lawn and garden. I see no one who could be Anna. But I need waxed floss, so I head to the toothbrush/toothpaste/oral care aisle.

On my way I see a woman in a blue vest in a heated discussion with a customer. A thirtysomething frizzy brunette in a dingy yellow halter top (no bra) and Daisy Dukes is pushing the Walmart employee with her index finger and loudly explaining why she opened a pack of diapers. "My kid shit his pants. You understand?"

In the customer's cart is a boy wearing a Pampers blue-and-white diaper and nothing else. Apparently his pants and shirt have been thrown away. I guess next stop: toddler clothes.

I with purposeful strides until I'm positioned between them, facing the cranky customer.

"Hey. Whoa, lady. Back up," I say. "Do not touch anybody. You understand me?"

"What the fuck you gonna do?" she says.

"I'm not telling *you* my next move. But I think you should start walking away."

"Ooh. Big tough guy. I'm shaking…"

I reach into my pocket and drop ten one-dollar bills into her cart. "Here," I say. "Get something for your baby. And then pay for it."

She grabs the cash and stares at me.

I turn to the employee, a gorgeous young woman who has her arms crossed. A blonde with blue eyes and full lips. "Let's walk away, okay?" I say. "It's not worth it." She's maybe twenty-five or twenty-six years old. I look at the nametag attached to the blue vest.

Wal-Mart

ANNA

Our People Make the Difference!

Oh my god. It's her.

"You're Anna!" I say, idiotically pointing at her nametag. "Can I talk to you for a minute?" I realize I seem much too eager.

"Look, sir, I appreciate your help, but I was handling it. I was going to tell her about resources where she can get free diapers and other items. And by the way, we have security." She sighs. "Anyway, how can I help you?"

"Your name is Anna Connor? Is that right? I'm Jack, by the way."

"Yes. That's my name," she says. I'm watching her mouth and am mesmerized with the movement of her tongue and lips as she enunciates *That's my name.* "Are you the guy with the thirty dollars?"

"Yes. Kinda. I mean, I don't owe you thirty dollars. I just didn't want to tell that manager my business. So I told him that I owe you money."

"What do you want?"

"Look, would you have lunch with me sometime? I would love to get to know you."

"Nope. Sorry. My boyfriend would not approve. I don't go out with men I don't know."

"Boyfriend?" I say. "He's not your fiancé?"

"No. We've only been dating two months or so, if that's any of your business."

"I'm happy to give you thirty dollars if you'll have lunch with me. Public place. Wherever you like." I pause. "Boyfriend's name is Tom?"

She narrows her eyes. "How do you know that? Dude, you are creeping me out. Seriously."

"Do you live on Idaho Street?"

"Dude, you need to leave. Please. I have to work. And for your information, I have never lived on that street. And I will *not* tell you where I live."

"Okay. Okay. Just one sec." I write my name, email address, and phone number on the back of a Sears receipt and hand it to her. "Look, I have an important message for you. And I can't just tell you here in the middle of Walmart. Call me. Please."

She takes the receipt and looks at it. "Three-one-four area code. Where are you from?"

"I live in Missouri. Just outside St. Louis, in St. Charles. About forty-five minutes from here. I have a house near historic Main Street, just around the corner from a Starbucks, where I spend a lot of time reading, writing… I'm an editor, and…" I'm now rambling.

"You have been driving forty-five minutes each way—from another state—to find me to give me a message? How long did it take you to find me?"

"Well, I thought it was going to be more difficult than it has turned out to be, even though I was told you probably worked at this Walmart. Your name is quite common, you see, so I was worried it would be hard to find you. I kind of felt like the Terminator trying to find Sarah Connor in Los Angeles. Did you see the movie? Arnold Schwarzenegger, the cybernetic assassin from the future, has to use a phone book—" I pause. I realize it's probably not a good idea to compare her with Sarah Connor and me with Arnold. Because that would make *me* the Terminator. When I'm really more like Reese. "Well, anyway, I started looking for you yesterday. But I've had this message since New Year's Day 2000."

"Dude, it's 2003. That message can't possibly be important anymore."

"I was told that the message would have no significance to you until at least the spring or summer of 2003. It's about something that could happen later this year—in the fall."

"The fall? This coming fall? You're not making any sense."

"Please, just call me when you have a free moment."

She looks at me. She is scared, clearly. And angry. She crosses her arms. "Please go."

I have fucked this up. "I'm sorry," I say.

I turn around and walk out of Walmart.

I know I have to play it cool for a while. I hope that she calls me, but it doesn't seem likely. Dating her now is impossible.

But I must get the message to her before summer.

In early May, I call the store and find out that the evening shift ends at 11:30 p.m. I'm not sure what days she works, but I drive to the Granite City Walmart on a Friday night at eleven p.m. and walk around inside. After ten minutes of wandering, I see her bagging at the registers, talking with customers. Big gorgeous smile. Then she turns and sees me. *Crap.*

I go back outside and walk around the back to see if employees have their own entrance. They don't. I will have to watch both front entrances.

At 11:31, workers in blue vests begin exiting. Anna

walks out escorted by an older man in a blue vest, and they turn left. They approach a red Jeep Cherokee. Older model. Maybe 1990. Illinois plates. Several small dents on the hood. She hops in, starts the engine, and rolls down the window. She waves to her coworker and drives off.

I decide to follow her. She pulls out of the lot and heads east on Pontoon Road. Suddenly I stop. *What am I doing?* Following her is a very bad idea, clearly. Creepy. Cringey. She told me that she does not live on Idaho. I have to believe her. I think I must wait for her to contact me.

I drive home.

The next afternoon, I receive an email from TJ2o9@hotmailcom.

Subject: Hey Asshole Back Off

Man stop stalking my girlfriend. My name is Tom.

And I'm officially warning you. Back off now.

I have not made a great first impression. …

Chapter Fifteen

June 19, 2003

I ROLL OVER and pick up my phone—my new Blackberry. It's been buzzing more than usual this morning. So maybe I need to be up. But I didn't go to bed until two a.m., and it's now, like, seven thirty.

I have four missed calls from a 618 number and an email from Anna37386@aol.com.

Subject: Hey Jack. Call me.

Hey Jack. I think I need to get that message from you. If there really is a message.

Call me. 618-555-8977

Anna Connor

She picks up on the first ring. "Hello?"

"Hi, Anna. It's Jack. Can you talk?"

"Yes. I'm at home. Alone."

"Are you still with the boyfriend?"

"Yes." She pauses. "Tom asked me to marry him a few weeks ago. I said yes."

"Okay. So he is now your fiancé," I say. "You never gave us a chance."

"Ha. You are so funny." She pauses. "I'm not sure how you predicted that I would have a fiancé this year. But that's not why I contacted you."

"Okay. What's going on?"

"Well, my future in-laws bought a house yesterday. 'Investment property' is what they are calling it. They say they can fix it up in a few weeks, install new carpets and such, and I can move in, rent-free. I don't make a lot at Walmart, so it's a huge help. Anyway, Tom will continue to live with them until the wedding. Then Tom will move into the house with me when we get married sometime next year."

"I think I know what you are going to say."

"Yeah. It's on Idaho Street. I don't know how you knew."

"It's complicated. Like quantum physics complicated. I just want to talk to you. I swear."

"I know. But I'm scared now."

"I mean, I get it. But trust me. Everything is going to be fine."

June 23, 2003

It's a gorgeous day. Seventy degrees and sunny. It's around six p.m., and I'm standing on the sidewalk outside Clark's restaurant on Main. I see Anna's red Jeep slow down as it passes Clark's. There's no parking available in this block, so she continues to drive. I walk down the sidewalk to meet her. She parallel parks in front of a print shop. When she turns off the engine, I notice that the wheels are almost three feet from the curb.

Anna walks around her Jeep, holding a lighter, her keys, and a pack of cigarettes. "Hi," she says.

"Are you going to leave your vehicle like that?" I say. "It needs to be closer to the curb."

She looks at the Jeep, turns back to me, tosses the keys in my direction, and says, "Go for it."

I catch the keys in my right hand. I repark the Jeep while she waits on the sidewalk. She lights a cigarette. As I step back onto the sidewalk, I toss the keys back to her, which are shoved into her jeans. She takes three quick puffs on her cigarette, blows smoke into the sky, stubs it out on the front tire of her Jeep, and puts the used cigarette back in the pack.

"Let's just sit out here on a bench," she says.

"Okay."

She really is quite lovely. Full lips, blue eyes with long lashes, radiant skin. A tongue to die for.

"If you want to grab dinner or a drink, let me know," I say. "This place is the best."

"No. I'm good." She tries to smile. She sits.

"Thanks for meeting me today," I say. "Look, I'm an

ordinary guy. Divorced. I have two beautiful daughters who are the world to me. I edit books. I like to ride my bike. I simply have been asked to give you a message. So please don't be nervous." I pause. And look into her eyes. She seems to relax a bit. "Can I ask you something?"

"Okay."

"This has nothing to do with the message. But somehow you look familiar. I've seen your face somewhere."

"Well, I did a bit of modeling in my teens. Nothing worth talking about. I posed for some department store ads. I was told to get braces, lose twenty-five pounds, and grow three inches in height. I did none of those things. Braces, as you might guess, are a bit expensive on Walmart wages. Or Bandanas wages. Or White Castle wages. I did lose five pounds by staying away from candy. And my height hasn't changed since age fifteen. I'm still five feet four."

"Okay. Well, I think your smile is quite lovely. None of those other things matter in the least."

"Can we talk about the message?"

"Sure. Look, Anna. I'm not supposed to tell you how I know about the Idaho Street house. And I want to be honest with you. I really do. But some things I cannot talk about. In December 1999, I received a message about you and for you. It said that you will get engaged this year: 2003. It mentioned your fiancé's name. Anyway, the message said that you become pregnant sometime in the late summer. Tom encourages you go to a family planning clinic in early November to have a procedure so that his parents don't freak out. You go through with it but feel intense guilt afterward. You get depressed. Smoke more. Then you and I meet for the first time in Decemb—"

"Wait. You're saying I'm going to meet you for the first time in December of this year? You do realize of course that I met you in April. And I would never get an abortion."

"Just let me finish, please. According to the message, we MET in late December. We HAD a relationship until February, when you ASKED me to leave you alone. I then WALKED out of your life forever. And you MARRIED Tom some time in 2004."

Anna just stares at me. Then says, "You are talking in the past tense."

"Yes." I pause. "Look," I say, "getting pregnant and then, you know, having the procedure apparently damages your relationship with him. It ruins your… It damages you. I was told to warn you. Encourage you to get on birth control and use condoms. Maybe if you and Tom get pregnant *after* the wedding, things will be better…"

"Mister, you're not making any sense. There is no way you can know these things. It's bullshit."

"Please call me Jack. Idaho Street, remember? I nailed it."

"Yeah. That's weird. But maybe my future in-laws have been looking at houses on Idaho since April. Maybe you are their real estate agent or something. Maybe my fiancé's parents are trying to scare me into being a good little girl… And I told you: I would not do that. We want to have kids. Tom wants to have boys. But you think you can walk in here and tell me this shit. You think you're some prince that needs to save me! Save the poor little girl from Walmart." She shakes her head. "You are such an ass."

"Come on. I'm not trying to—"

"Who is the message from?"

I look into her blue eyes. "I can't tell you that. You must trust me. Please. The message is from someone who cares about you."

"Tell. Me."

"Anna, it doesn't even matter. I'm not asking you to do something illegal. The message just says, *Hey, maybe take precautions.* Like, maybe you should remind Tom that he promised his parents that he would 'wait until marriage.' The message is so simple: *Be careful.*"

"Jack, you need to be honest with me. It sounds like the message is from a psychic or a fortune teller or from my deceased father. Please be honest with me. Honesty means more to me than anything else."

I hesitate. Telling her could be dangerous if we are being monitored. But I say, "Okay. But you must not repeat this to anyone." I pause again. "The message is from the year 2026."

She shakes her head and rolls her eyes. "2026? In twenty-three years humankind has the ability to send messages back in time. But instead of, say, killing Hitler or telling Hitler's dad to use a condom, they decide to tell a lady at Walmart that she needs to use one."

"Look, I don't make the rules. I simply received the message."

"How did you receive the message? Postcard? A séance? Morse code?"

"I received an email."

"An email? Of course. It's nice to know that email is still a thing in 2026. From whom?"

"Me. The email is from me."

"Ha-ha! You are so funny." She laughs. Then frowns. "And so full of it. Does the I-have-a-message-from-the-future line work on many women? Do me a favor and send a message back to yourself. Please let your *future* self know that I won't be having a fling with you in December. Or now. Or in any other time or dimension. Then get into your time machine and go to the planet Mars."

"Anna, first of all, I can't send any messages to the future," I say. "It's just not possible." I pause. "And I'm not sure how you know about the trip to Mars."

She shakes her head with contempt and rises from the bench and walks back to her perfectly parked Jeep. She starts the Jeep, revs the engine, and takes off.

Okay. So she doesn't believe me. But maybe the thought has been planted in her head, like: *What if I do get pregnant? What would happen? What would Tom say? What would we do?*

Maybe she'll be careful. Insist on condoms. Get the pill. Do something to change her future.

Chapter Sixteen

October 3, 2003

I ROLL OVER IN BED and wonder why it's so cold in my bedroom… And then I remember: *This is not my bedroom. Not my bed. Not my house.* I push myself to the edge of the mattress and very carefully slide myself off the bed without waking… her. Jody, I think. Or Joan. Joanie! Well, I don't know, honestly; but I think she works as a teacher and has a Jaguar.

Suddenly, my Blackberry is vibrating. And it's at 4 percent battery. And a call is coming in from … "ANNA CONNOR."

I grab my clothes and tiptoe down a hallway and into a very small bathroom. I tap Accept. "Hi, Anna. How are you?"

"Jack, why are you whispering? Never mind. Can you come over? I need someone to talk to." She has been crying. I can hear it in her voice.

"I can come over later, around two thirty a.m. After my part-time job. Is that okay?"

"Yes. That's fine. Tom will be at work until six a.m. My address is 2215 Idaho Street, if you don't know that already."

"I guess I do. I looked it up."

"Wonderful. See you at two thirty, then. And don't park directly in front of the house."

October 4, 2003

Granite City, Illinois, is in the so-called Metro East area just east of St. Louis. It was founded as a steel-making city. And it is still mostly a steel town. Idaho Street is in the center of the city (just a few blocks from downtown), about a mile from the steel mills on Horse-shoe Lake. Anna's house is close enough to the steel factories that I can smell the sulfur and other steel-making byproducts in the air.

I get directions from MapQuest and pull onto Idaho Street around 2:40 a.m. I park a block away and keep scanning, checking to make sure no one is following me or watching the house. The porch light is off, but light is coming from the living room window.

I tap on the front door.

I can see Anna get up from the couch and walk toward the front door. A TV is on across from the couch.

"Hey," says Anna. "Come on in. I'm going to close the blinds and drapes. If one of Tom's friends drives by,

I want them to think I'm asleep." Anna is wearing baggy sweatpants and a gray long-sleeve T-shirt. She's barefoot.

I walk in and stand in the foyer. I watch as Anna closes the drapes in the living room. She turns off the table lamp. She mutes the TV. To the left of the TV is a bookshelf. I see *To Kill a Mockingbird*, some Stephen King, Salinger, Nabokov, Agatha Christie, Annie Proulx, some bodice-ripper romance, even some gay romance.

"Have a seat. Tom let me know when I moved in here that he has friends keeping an eye on the house. To make sure I'm 'safe.'" Anna makes air quotes and rolls her eyes. "He is very jealous. He doesn't trust me apparently." She pauses and down looks at my hands. "What is that?"

I suddenly remember I'm holding a package. It's a present wrapped in beige paper decorated with green and gold leaves.

"Oh. Present for you." I hand it to her and she places it on the coffee table.

I sit on the couch. Anna sits at the other end. She puts her bare feet on the edge of the coffee table. And I find myself looking at her toes. No nail polish. But gorgeous piggies.

"Tell me about your library," I say.

"Library? You mean my particleboard bookshelf? Ha. I love books. I've recently been reading bodice-ripping romance and gay men's romance. You believe it? I get so turned on."

"Why gay romance novels?"

"Hmm. I think because it's rough and passionate.

Men can't hide their desire, if you know what I mean. And the descriptions of the men… wow. Two well-endowed men who are so—"

"Whoa! Is it getting hot in here?"

She is quiet for a moment. "Jack… I'm pregnant," she says.

"Well, did—"

"Look, Jack, I'm sure. I took the test three times. I started with the dollar-store test. I ended up buying a Clearblue two-pack. I'm such an idiot. You told me to be careful. And I got the pill too. I took it every day. I swear. And Tom hates condoms of course. He swears to me that he always pulls out in time."

"Does Tom know?"

"No. But Jack, I know he wants to have kids. I *know* that."

"But…?"

"But I'm scared. Because your predictions have been spot on." She pauses and moves closer to me. "What if I don't tell him right away? Try to hide the baby bump when I start to show. And maybe if he doesn't see the bump right away, it will be too late to have the procedure."

"Maybe that would work," I say. I watch her. I stare at her perfect lips. "Or maybe just tell him that abortion is off the table."

She shakes her head. "If I wait until I'm showing, he will be so mad that I lied to him for months." She pauses. "His parents are religious. They will be so judgmental. I know it. They will be mortified."

"Maybe the bump will make the baby more real to

him. Maybe he will want you to keep the baby. And to hell with his mom and dad. If you tell Tom that an abortion will devastate you, he will figure out a way to tell his parents."

"Jack, you don't know him. But your future self apparently does. In 2026, your future self gets to send you one email, and the message is about me. It was important. *I* was very important."

"The message had several major parts. But yes, I think this was an important part of the message. He certainly wanted you to be happy. And having met you, I get that."

She looked at me. "You *get* that?"

"Yes. Look, I'm not going to hit on you. Our fling in the other timeline clearly made the problems between you and Tom bigger—worse. But I can see why my future self fell for you. You are gorgeous and good. And clearly you love that baby. I have two daughters. The younger one was born in 1992. My older daughter was born in August 1989. She was conceived in November 1988. If my future self could only send a message to October 1988, he would have refused because the mere opening of the email would have changed my life's trajectory such that my daughters' conceptions would no longer be assured. Instead of having a redhead girl, I might have had a son named Dylan; instead of a curly-headed girl named Envie, I might have a blond boy named Milton who looks like me, or maybe twins or no children at all. The future Jack O'Donnell would not have risked losing Envie and Joy."

"But your future self wanted me to know that my

first child was at risk of being killed by their own father."

"I wouldn't put it like that. Family planning clinics exist for a reason—some young couples aren't ready to—"

"'Family planning'? Bullshit, Jack. You know what happened. In another timeline, Tom persuaded me to… to… And I went along with it."

"I only told you to be careful because in the other timeline your love for Tom made you do something that harmed you. It damaged you."

Anna is quiet. Then she says, "Why did you bring me a present?"

"I felt that you might need something to cheer you up. You sounded down."

Anna is already unwrapping the present. She pulls away the paper and reveals a cardboard box the size of a Kleenex box. She opens the top. She reaches in and pulls out three pairs of white socks for a newborn and a tiny white onesie that reads: BEST BABY EVER.

Anna begins to cry. "Jack… I… You knew."

"I had a feeling that you might be… ya know. I'm finding that it's not so easy to change the future. And clearly, the fact that you were on the pill makes this baby very special."

Anna looks down and continues to cry.

"Anna, why are you crying?"

"These are happy tears, I guess. This time, I know that I will give birth to this baby."

"Anna..."

"What, Jack?"

"There is no such thing as 'happy tears.' When people say 'Oh, these are happy tears,' they are lying. In my experience, so-called happy tears means the person does not feel worthy to be happy. Or the person believes that happiness is always fleeting and short-lived or followed by suffering. Anna, you deserve happiness. You deserve the blessings that this baby will give you. Tom needs to understand that you need this. You deserve this. It is your body. It is your child."

Anna is quiet for several minutes. "Jack, you know, if your future self fell in love with me in December 2003, you could love me now. Two months earlier."

"Whoa," I say. "I never said 'love.' Who said 'love'? It was an affair. I thought I made it clear that I'm not going to do that this time. Anna Connor in the other timeline likely fell for Jack simply to get even with Tom. But if you can get Tom to accept this pregnancy—and the baby—you'll have a shot at a much better marriage." And I know that my future self did love her very much. And I am falling for her. *But beautiful women always walk, don't they?*

"Jack still loves me in 2026," Anna says. "In 2026, it's like he freed a genie from a bottle and got three wishes. He used one of those wishes on me and my happiness. You know that Jack loved me. You knew even before you met me. He mentioned it in the email, didn't he?"

"You got pregnant. You and *Tom* are having a baby. So now *you* are in charge of your happiness and your future. If you want to keep this baby, you must stand up to Tom and tell him that." I look at the TV. It's an *X-*

Files rerun, the episode in which a scientist travels into the past to destroy his own research on time travel. *What the fuck.*

"Before I tell Tom," she says, breaking me away from the TV, "I need to know if there is anything between us. If we have chemistry. If we have feelings for each other."

"What?! No, Anna. You are going about this in the wrong order. Talk to Tom and see what he says. I'll still be around. Look, Jack may have loved you in the other timeline. It's possible. Well, it's more than possible. Okay, maybe Jack *was* crazy about you…"

Anna pulls off the T-shirt and drops it on the couch. She's wearing a tan bra, a nice one that immediately draws my attention.

"And speaking of bodice-ripping…"

"Do you want to rip off anything?" she says. "You are very cute. I noticed that when I met you at Walmart."

"Anna," I say, pulling my gaze up to hers, "we need to slow down before this goes any further. Do not make me walk out of here. If you love Tom, talk to him."

"Do you like me?" she says.

"Well, yes. I do. You are a sweetheart. You are a beauty… drop-dead gorgeous. And busty of course."

"Ha. Yes. I've been busty since I was thirteen. It drove my parents crazy. Lots of older guys wanted to date me when I was in middle school."

"Well, I'm sure your dad kept an eye on you."

"True. Dad often said that I reached 'critical mass' way too young. He said that if I were ever left alone with a boy, it could cause a chain reaction that might be dangerous."

"Your dad had a way with words. Did he work at a nuclear power plant?"

"I don't want to talk about my dad. Come into the kitchen with me," Anna says.

That sounds safer than sitting next to her on the couch, so I follow her down a dark hallway. The kitchen is mostly dark, but there is light coming from a doorway on the far side of the room. I can make out the kitchen table, four chairs, the sink. I can smell maple syrup. I see a pack of Marlboro Lights on the table.

"By the way, Anna, you need to quit smoking. I once used Wellbutrin—"

"I'm not smoking another cigarette. I promise. But getting rid of the cigarette packs would make Tom suspicious." She looks into my eyes. She puts her hands on my shoulders. "Here. Stand on this side of the kitchen table," she says. "I'll stand on the other side."

Suddenly we are on opposite sides of the small table. It's maybe four feet wide. She reaches out her hands to me.

"Hold my hands across the table. You must stay on that side. I must stay on this side."

"Are you going to put your shirt back on?" I ask.

"Ha-ha. Not yet. I want you to lean toward me and kiss me. Remember, things can't go too far because we are staying on opposite sides of this table. Okay?"

I'm suddenly no longer thinking with my brain. "All right. I think kissing you would be very nice. But you are going to want to meet with Tom and see how he feels about the baby."

"Shhh," says Anna. "Lean toward me. Like this." Anna lets go of my hands, places her hands on the table, closes her eyes, and leans forward over the table. She puckers her lips just barely.

I meet her in the middle. I close my eyes. And we kiss. Tenderly. Haltingly. I lean farther, kissing her cheeks and her neck, breathing in the scent of her hair. I kiss her shoulder. And then our mouths are back together. I hear moaning and realize it is me. I want the table to disappear. Everything else seems to fall away. It's just me and Anna and this goddammed table.

She pulls away. "Jack, I don't like this."

It takes me a moment to comprehend her words. "Mmm. What?!" I open my eyes. "Why is that?"

"The table is keeping you from holding me. I'm leaning forward as far as I can."

I smile. "Yes. I'll admit that I'd rather you were leaning over something else."

"What's that?"

"Your bed. With me behind you."

Anna giggles. "Oh my. That would be fun." She grabs my face and brings my lips to hers. It's almost slow motion. Her lips brush mine from side to side. Then she sighs and licks my lips. I am dizzy. Our lips come together and my breathing rate increases. Our tongues are suddenly entwined. And my cock swells in my jeans.

I put my hands in her hair, and I pull away for a moment. I need to stop before the desire overwhelms me. "Anna, the email said that you are an amazing singer."

"It does? I think I want to read that email."

"Sing something for me."

"Hmm. Okay. *When I'm in your arms, my loving heart beats like a drum / When you're in my mouth, I start to hum.*" She laughs.

"Oh my gosh. Aren't you naughty." I kiss her again. And it is so good it makes me high. I think, *I would do anything for you, Anna.* I lean in to kiss her again.

But now Anna pulls back. "Jack, why did your future self never look for me after I ended it?"

"He tried looking for you in 2014. You were still married. So he decided to not make contact."

"I mean before that. And after." She pauses. "Forget it. It doesn't matter now. I don't want to be married to Tom in 2014 or 2013 or 2004. The easiest way to avoid that scenario is to not get married in the first place."

"You're going to call off the wedding?" I ask.

"I'm calling it off now."

"But Tom will—"

"Tom will want to be rid of me when I tell him I've been making love to another man."

"What?!" Then I get it. "Oh. Well, remember, you have two wonderful young boys…"

"I can still have kids. In fact, I'm going to have one in seven months. Nothing can change my mind. No matter how many times you make love to me."

"I never said that I love you or will make love to you." *I didn't, did I?* "Look, yes, maybe my future self wanted a second chance with you. But he's not here. I haven't even had a first chance—" I suddenly realize that I've been in this room before. Or, rather, my future self has been in this room. I can feel it. My future self fell in love with Anna in this room. And somehow, once again, I feel unable to change the timeline. I need to change the timeline.

"Your first chance is now, silly. *Our* first chance is now. You keep saying that you don't love me, but I don't believe you. When you kiss me… oh my god, Jack. When you're not talking, your lips don't lie. Your lips tell me that you want me more than anything. Your lips give me more passion than I have ever known. Your eyes too. When you breathe on my neck, I want you inside me."

"Anna, I goofed. I should have begun looking for you before you met Tom. I didn't. Now Tom is involved." I pause. "Look, I can't promise I'll love you in the future. You can't promise that you will love me forever. That's why they invented divorce. Even though I've had a glimpse at one possible future, I can't just step into that future. All we have is this moment. I have one email from a man who clearly never got the hang of living in the now. And that man is me."

"You sent a message back in time. For me. And for you. That proves it to me. I don't need to hear it from your lips. Not yet. I know that if this table was not here and you held me in your arms, you would not be able to say 'I don't love you.'"

"Anna—"

"You can't do it. When you kiss me, you love me. You don't even need that email to convince you. You do.

And when you go to bed tonight, you will lie awake imagining me in your arms. You will fantasize about me. In your mind, we will be skin to skin. Your heart rate will increase. In your dreams you will make love to me."

Yes, I know.

"The email does suggest that he loved you. I am…"

I am… what? Falling in love with her? Of course I am. I'm the same person who fell for her in the other timeline. "Look, Tom may not want to give you up. You *are* having his baby."

Anna is quiet for a moment. She looks into my eyes. "I don't want him to know. And if he finds out I'm pregnant, I want him to believe it's not his."

"Anna, believe me. I want to take you to the bedroom right now and…" I trail off. "But you have a fiancé. Tell Tom it's over, and I'll be back. You can tell him you kissed me. Or that I kissed you. But until you take off that ring and give it back to Tom, this—" I gesture from me to her "—can't go any further. And do not tell Tom that this has anything to do with a message from the future. I don't want to be disappeared."

"Jack, look at my left hand."

I look down at her lovely hand. There is no ring.

"I took off the engagement ring yesterday."

Suddenly, I realize that I want to kiss her again. And I know that if I do, I will feel an urgency, a desire so strong that I will pull her over the table. I will pull off her bra and cover her breasts with kisses, and I will make love to her on this table. Unless she says no. And she won't. I push away. "Anna…" I kiss her on the forehead and turn around.

"You're leaving?"

"I am. Talk to Tom." And I walk out of her house on Idaho Street. And it's like I can't catch my breath. It feels like the hardest thing I have ever done.

Chapter Seventeen

October 8, 2003

I THOUGHT THAT I would hear from Anna within a day or two. That she would break up with Tom and then call me. But it's been four days. Nothing. I feel I need to see her. Something is wrong.

I get into my car and head to the Starbucks near my house. I order a latte. I sit down and open my laptop and check email. There is one email from Anna.

Subject: "I Told Tom About the Baby."

Damn.

Jack,
He knew somehow. Maybe he saw the pregnancy test in the trash. Or he noticed the prenatal vitamins.

Or maybe because my breath no longer smells like an ashtray and I no longer want him touching me. Like at all. I told him to stay away.

So he begged to come over. He sat on the couch and cried and begged me to tell him if I was pregnant. So I told him…everything. He forgave me for keeping it from him. He forgave me for letting you into the house. Into my life. He said he loves me. Tried to hug me, but I pulled away. I swear.

We went out for breakfast. My favorite place. Then he drove us to East St. Louis. He pleaded with me to go into Planned Parenthood and talk about options. We went in and received twelve pages of forms to fill out. I took the clipboard and began writing. Then we waited. I didn't know what to do. A nurse called me over but asked Tom to stay in the waiting area.

Pregnant?

I nodded.

She got my name and weight, scanned my driver's license and insurance card, then took my blood pressure, oxygen sat, heart rate, etc. She asked me about birth control, my diet, last menstrual period, and then she said something like, Do ya smoke, take any meds?

No, I said. I quit smoking the day my test showed the plus sign.

Then a bunch of rapid-fire questions: Are ya feeling well today? Any symptoms of cold or flu? Are ya safe? Is anyone forcing ya to be here today?

I said that I mostly felt okay. Some nausea, ya know?

Nausea is to be expected, blah blah.

But I'm not safe, I said. My baby is not safe. My fiancé wants me to terminate. But this time, I'm saying no.

This time?

Never mind. Look, I want to have my baby.

The nurse suddenly looked pretty fucking alarmed. She picked up a phone, pressed a key, and said, I need security in triage. Yep. Right now. She removed her lanyard and necklace and earrings.

She asked me to follow her right then.

So I followed her down a hall and into a windowless room.

Anna, I'm locking ya in her for just a few minutes. I'll be back when your fiancé has been escorted from the building. Are ya okay?

Yes, I said. Thank you.

So I guess security took Tom out of the building. I still need to get an order of protection or something.

A volunteer gave me a ride home.

Jack, please don't stop by the house on Idaho. Don't contact Tom. I'm okay. I've got some things I need to do.

XO Anna

Chapter Eighteen

October 10, 2003 (Columbus Day)

I GET UP AT NINE a.m. and send texts to Anna. I do not receive an instant reply. So I shower, get dressed. I grab my backpack and head over to Starbucks.

Now I'm sitting in Starbucks on October 10, 2003, 511 years after Christopher Columbus set foot in the Americas. I decide to read a bit about Columbus. I google "Christopher Columbus 1492."

After weeks at sea, Columbus landed in the Bahamas in the early-morning hours of October 12, 1492. He knelt on the ground and kissed the earth. Gave thanks to God. He was off course by thousands of miles, but he'd still found paradise.

I sip my latte and read. Soon I begin proofreading the page proofs retrieved from my backpack. I tune out the conversations around me.

This Starbucks is on the first floor of a five-story office building. They have beautiful, large wooden tables and good lighting. No drive-thru at this location. I can be found here most weekdays from, say, ten a.m. to around 4:15 p.m. Typically, I sit near a window, nursing a grande caramel macchiato while proofreading pages of a novel, a text on nursing, or maybe a self-improvement book.

On this particular day, I'm proofreading a science fiction novel, a dystopian fantasy set in a postapocalyptic world—earth. The writing is top shelf. Either that or the copy editor has gone above and beyond. However, there are a few misspellings here and there. With the movement of my red pencil, I change the figurative *further* to the literal *farther*. I decide to change "bare gut" to "bare abdomen." Then I read "A woman screamed mutely in pain or grief…" *Well*, I think, *I'm not sure how one can scream "mutely."* Suddenly, I remember the day I lifted binoculars to my eyes and saw a woman screaming, mutely, some seventy feet away, her voice silenced by double-pane windows and morning traffic fourteen floors below. Mutely. Screaming. And then her head was shoved face first into a pillow on the hotel bed.

Maybe I will just query the editor on this point. Or maybe I should let it go.

"Hey there." It's a woman's voice, very close. A pretty voice. A familiar voice. I place my pencil next to my grande cup and look up from my work. It's Anna, but today she is wearing makeup, lipstick, and her hair is carefully arranged. She smiles. "That looks like *fun*," she says. "What are you doin'?"

I smile as I take in her smile, her eyes. She's wearing a black, skin-tight T-shirt and form-fitting blue jeans.

She's holding a paperback novel in one hand and venti-sized coffee drink in the other.

"I'm proofreading a novel. Science fiction," I say. "How did you find me?"

"Starbucks. Near historic Main Street, St. Charles. You spend a lot of time here, or so you say. Hey, don't mind me. You keep working." She smiles, leans over and points at my page proof, specifically the change from *further* to *farther*. "Great catch." She stands, backs up two steps, turns, and walks to an upholstered chair twenty feet away. She sits down, places her coffee on an end table, opens her book, crosses her legs, and reads.

I look at my phone. 4:02 p.m. *Damn. I have to leave in fifteen minutes.* She lifts her head and looks at me for about three seconds.

I collate my page proofs, slip a rubber band around them, and stow my pencils and laptop. I pick up my backpack and walk to her.

"What are you reading?" I ask.

She looks up at me. "Hmm. It's sort of a romance-adventure."

I notice that there is still no ring on her left hand. "Yeah. I'm here most weekdays. Late morning to around four fifteen. I have another job in the evenings, Anna. UPS. In fact, I have to leave in ten minutes."

"Today is a federal holiday, though. Columbus Day, the second Monday in October. You have to work at UPS?" She frowns.

I look at my phone: 4:10. "Unfortunately, yes, I have to work on Columbus Day."

"That's okay. I should have called first."

I hold up a finger. "Hold on a sec." I pull out my phone and tap out a number.

"Twilight office. Jason."

"Hi, Jason. It's Jack O'Donnell. I'm afraid I can't make it in tonight."

"You're calling in thirty minutes before your shift?"

"Very sorry. I can't make it in."

Click. Jason hung up. I turn back to Anna.

"Let's do dinner tonight."

"Awesome. I'm single, Jack. And pregnant. And it's all good. No more 'happy tears.' I'm going to have a beautiful baby. And I'm genuinely happy."

"I'm very glad, Anna. By the way, you look amazing. You look happy."

"Jack, if you had not sought me out and told me my future, I know I would have…" She looks down for a moment, then raises her face and looks into my eyes. "Tom had power over me. I can almost see him manipulating…" She pauses and seems to stifle a sob. "But you saved me. You saved this child inside me. So in a way, she is yours. I'm not saying you are the father, of course. But in my heart, you will always be her dad. Because you loved her mom enough to save her."

"'She'? 'Her'? How do you know it's a girl?"

"I just know somehow." She pauses. "I'm going to get a small coffee. You need anything?"

"I'm good."

Anna walks to the counter to order.

I sit down. As I look toward the entrance, a woman named Jane walks in. "Hey, Jack!" she calls out. Jane is a regular… usually gets a venti Iced Caramel Macchiato with almond milk and an extra shot of espresso. Extra caramel drizzle on top of the foam, with light ice. Or something like that.

I freeze. I look at Jane. Then Anna.

Crap.

"Hey, Jane!"

She stops in front of me and spreads her arms for a hug. I stand up and hug her like she's my aunt or sister.

"How are you doing, Jack? Don't you need to be at work?"

"I'm good. Skipping work tonight. You?" Anna is smiling at me.

"I'm good. I need coffee," Jane says.

She walks to another table and hugs another man and kisses him on the cheek.

My phone vibrates. I reach into my pocket, pull it out, and look down.

I think I want to kiss you.

I smile. Anna walks to me. And we do kiss. "I may need to keep an eye on you."

"Jane is something of a Starbucks barfly… a Starfly."

"Ever date her?"

"I wouldn't call it a date."

Chapter Nineteen

October 11, 2003

THE NEXT DAY I do go into work at UPS.

During the day, I sort and re-sort words, putting letters, commas, periods, parentheses, verbs, nouns, sentences, paragraphs, and chapters in the right order. A book is simply a big filing cabinet.

At night, I sort boxes, packages. I am a part-time sorter at the UPS. I get shitty pay but unbelievably fantastic benefits—health insurance, dental, vision, mental health, 401(k).

Tonight I am sorting boxes from the Scholastic Book Club. The unloader is in a 53-foot trailer that contains 8,500 boxes of books. He is dropping the boxes on the belt at a brisk pace, about one box every second. I toss a box addressed to Dallas TX 75241 to the tan belt. Houston TX 77041 goes to the black belt. Columbia MO 65212, tan. San Francisco, pink. Idaho, pink.

Maine, gray. Kansas City, blue. Second Day Air package to Mississippi, gold. Atlanta, orange. St. Louis MO 63115, red. St. Louis MO 63141, green… Toss, toss, drop, toss, drop and kick, hook shot, toss…

"Hey, Jack." I look up. Ben, my supervisor, is headed my way. I push my iPod headband above my ears, and I continue to toss boxes.

"Jack, keep up the pace. You are doing great. The unload supervisor says you're doing twenty-three hundred for the first hour."

"You're actually admitting that I'm doing twenty-three hundred packages per hour?" I ask. "Then why do I see reports that show I am doing twelve hundred an hour?"

"Jack, twelve hundred is an average for this section. I can't spend my time counting packages per hour for everyone."

"Maybe you could count my speed for, say, a minute, and then multiply by sixty."

"Yeah, maybe. Just keep up the pace."

I readjust my headband. My iPod is pumping out disco tunes, rock, dance stuff, Motown, Britney, Pink Floyd. During the second half of my four-hour shift, I switch to an audiobook: *The Time Traveler's Wife.*

At the end of Chapter 4, I turn off the iPod, thinking about *The Time Traveler's Wife*. Then I think about Anna. I believe that we belong together this time. *In this time.*

Chapter Twenty

October 17, 2003

ANNA AND I CONTINUE to text and talk over the next several days. Tom has reminded Anna that the house belongs to his parents. He is staying away, but his patience is wearing thin. If they do not reconcile, she could be out of the house soon.

I decide to skip my UPS job. I'm on deadline. I'm proofreading a book of essays and stories about growing up gay in North Carolina. I arrive at Starbucks at five p.m. and plan to stay until I finish my proofreading project or until closing, which is nine p.m.

Around seven p.m. I notice that Footnote Cymbals' "Cry These Tears on My Own" is playing in the background. I close my eyes and listen.

I watched you walking away
While I begged you to stay

Now I see your face in my mind
Dreaming of the winter when you were mine
You said you saw love in my eyes
As I kissed you from shoulders to thighs
But I'll cry these tears on my own.

I tried calling your phone
But it's on silent when he's home
Now I know it's the end
Will never know where you went
You once needed my love
You once pleaded, my love
Now I'll cry these tears on my own
Yes, I need to cry these tears on my own

When I open my eyes, a thirtysomething blonde is walking in carrying a backpack and a folder and asks me if she can sit across from me at the large, gorgeous walnut table where I often sit. "Sure," I say. She drops her backpack and folder on the table. She heads to the counter and buys a latte and returns; she sits, facing me. She grades papers ("These are middle school essays," she says to me) and chuckles occasionally and flexes her neck by dipping her head left and right. We engage in small talk from time to time. I tell her I am a freelance proofreader and copy editor.

"Oh. Neat. I don't want to bother you, but maybe you would give me your opinion on this essay. It's kind of funny."

"Okay. I'm Jack, by the way."

"Carol," she says.

Instead of handing it to me, she reads the essay out loud.

I say, "Yeah. That's pretty bad. Although, for middle school, maybe that's not the worst you have seen."

I can't give much of an assessment by listening to a paper. I can't see it. Can't see the spelling, the punctuation. My skill is reading: reading sentences word by word with my bespectacled eyes. It's the way I get stuff into my brain. I can then transpose words and phrases, insert and delete punctuation, correct grammar. Fix danglers and modifiers.

"I'm doing this substitute teaching job," she says. "Private school. My dad is getting so tired of supporting me. I also work at a gym."

"Hmm," I say.

"I used to be a dancer. Musical theater, Broadway-type shows. I performed on a cruise ship for three years. The contract called for two shows a day, six days a week, for ten months straight."

"I can see you as a dancer," I say. She is thin and toned, pretty face, pale complexion. A sharp, slightly large nose. Sort of reminds me of Carole King. *I've seen her before. Probably here.*

"Thank you. Let me tell you, when you board a cruise ship for a ten-month gig, you must get a boyfriend within the first two days. No, the first day, actually. Otherwise, they are all taken. I spent that first year stealing time from other performers' boyfriends."

"I see. I never thought about that." I smile.

I look back down and proof my pages, check email on my laptop. Drink latte. Carol has stopped grading papers and is now stretching. She stretches the upper trapezius for a few moments and then does an eagle pose that stretches the shoulder blades. I think she wants me to comment. But I don't.

At 8:58, the barista walks over to our table and quietly mentions that Starbucks is "closing in two minutes." I gather my stuff and put everything in my backpack. Carol stands. She is waiting. We walk to the door. "Where are you heading?" she asks.

"I don't know. Maybe Borders. Or Denny's. Maybe home." We walk to the parking lot, side by side.

She says, "I would love to hang out with you."

"Hmm. Okay."

"Are you going to Borders to work?" she asks.

"Hmm. I think I'm done working for tonight. Maybe we should go to Denny's?"

"Go together in your car? Is that okay?"

"Sure," I say. "My car is just around the block, at my house."

I look at her from the side. She tilts her head and there is a hint of a smile.

"But you know, you have to make a choice," she says.

"What's that?"

"We can be friends. *Or* we can have a… one-night stand." She grins and looks into my eyes.

"Really?" I say. I pause, looking at her mouth, her eyes. "I guess we will be friends, then."

We continue walking. Then I stop and look straight ahead.

"What's wrong?" says Carol, turning and looking up at me.

"If we go to Denny's, I'm probably going to find that you are charming and sexy (well, I already know that you are sexy) and… I'll probably take you home later. I'm sure of it. And I can't do that. I'm seeing someone. And while I haven't made any promises to her, I guess I'm making some promises to myself. My future self." I suddenly realize how much I want to see Anna.

"Future self? Hmm. Whatever. Goodnight, Jack." Carol turns and walks away.

I know that my free time should be spent with Anna. I want her next to me.

Chapter Twenty-One

November 1, 2003

"I BOUGHT THE HOUSE a few years ago," I say, opening the front door and letting Anna walk inside. "Right after the divorce, I moved in with my dad. Within four months I'd saved enough for the down payment. My first priority was the fixing the wiring and the HVAC. Then painting the girls' rooms. Then painting the living room and working on the floor. Now I'm working on the floor in the dining room. The entire first floor is about nine hundred square feet and mostly hardwood except for the kitchen. In the dining room, I've had to pull up the carpet, pads, thousands of staples, and then there was linoleum under the carpet. The linoleum had been glued to Masonite, which was nailed and stapled to the hardwood floors. The dining room floor was in terrible shape—scratches, dings, stains, nail holes. But I spend at least two hours a day sanding them with a belt sander. I think they will be pretty when I am done."

"I love old houses," Anna says as we walk through the first floor.

I switch on lights in the kitchen. "As you can see," I say, "the kitchen was updated in the early seventies. By a family on a limited budget."

We walk into the dining room.

"I can see what you mean by the floors. They will be gorgeous."

I step over a tool box. "Watch your step." I turn on a table lamp. "I love the fireplace. I have used it a couple of times, but there is something wrong with the flue. It gets a little smoky in here. And I have a gas fireplace in my bedroom."

We ascend the stairs and make a right turn into my bedroom. I flick on the light.

"Blue carpeting, I see," she says. "Cerulean blue. Interesting."

"Yes. I'll change that eventually. I don't have hardwood floors in here, so I'll get some new carpeting when I can afford it."

"This room is huge."

"Twelve by twenty-six."

She looks at my bed. "Do you mind if I lie down for a bit? Maybe take a little nap?"

"Sure. Go ahead," I say, putting my hands on my hips. I'm not sure what else to say.

Anna kicks off her boots and gets under the covers and scoots to the far side of the bed. There is suddenly movement under the covers. She's taking off some clothing. Her jeans, apparently. Then she rolls onto her side and closes her eyes, facing me. I stand there for a moment, and then say, "I'll turn off the light."

"No. That's okay. It's not that bright in here."

I head to the bathroom. And I ponder what to do. I stand there, looking in the mirror, then I brush my teeth, and go into the hallway, just outside my bedroom. I look in. Her head is on the pillow, but her eyes are open.

"Don't just stand there. Come lie with me."

I kick off my cowboy boots, peel off my socks, unfasten my belt, and take off my jeans. I get under the covers and face her.

"You are a good kisser," Anna says.

I laugh. "It's my specialty." I move closer, and we kiss. Then kiss again.

Anna smiles, then becomes serious. "Don't you dare take off your boxers unless you are wearing a condom."

I laugh again. "Well, I can't put one on until I am, *ahem*, aroused."

"Just so you understand," she says. "You can't even come close to my crotch area without a condom."

"Really? There are some in the nightstand if and when it becomes necessary."

She flips over and faces the wall. "Hold me," she whispers.

I spoon her and place my hand on her hip. My hand is on her panties and partly on her skin. Arousal seems imminent.

She presses her backside into my boxers. My erection is growing between her ass cheeks. A few minutes later, she says, "I can't sleep." Then: "You know, there is something you can do without a condom."

"What's that?"

"Oral."

"Mmm. Yes. Do you mind if I take off these covers?"

She sits up and kicks the duvet to the bottom of the bed. Her legs are yummy and smooth. But my eyes are drawn to her panties—a diaphanous, sparkly thong from Victoria's Secret. She takes off her sweater and then unfastens her bra with one hand. The bra falls into her lap.

"Damn!" I say.

"What?"

"Gorgeous breasts."

"Thank you." She scoots out of her panties and hands them to me. I put them to my face and breathe.

"Oh my god," I say.

I remove my shirt and lie on my back. Anna straddles my chest, holding onto the headboard. With my hands on her ass, I guide her closer to my face. I kiss her thighs, abdomen, and then her soft mound of curly blond hair.

I suck, kiss, and nibble her thighs and guide her private beach to my mouth. I inhale her scent and I get hard. Wide-mouthed, I moisten the labia, kissing deeply. My tongue finds the smoothest, most fragrant skin, just beyond the lips. She begins to thrust against my mouth. I get into sync with her movements and extend my tongue to match her thrusts with long strokes. I guide two fingers into her as my tongue, moving back and forth, then up and down, massages and stimulates the nub of flesh.

"Oh, yes," she moans. "Put a condom on. Please."

I tear open a package. With one hand I slip on a condom as she turns toward the foot of the bed, bends over, her face on the duvet and her ass up in the air.

I kiss her backside, lick her vadge one more time, and enter her. She gasps.

Her moans are intoxicating. And I suddenly realize that I am moaning, too. I find a pace and rhythm that makes her moans louder, more desperate, and I push into her over and over, cupping her breasts in my hands and alternately watching her backside bounce and glide onto me. The sound of our bodies slapping reminds me of running in flip-flops on the beach. I close my eyes and can still see our bodies moving together. Her core sliding back and forth on me. And I am harder than I have ever been.

I lick my thumb and push it gently into her asshole.

"Mmmm. I like that."

"Do you want me in your ass?"

"Don't even think about it." She turns to glare at me and then kisses me over her shoulder. "Next time. Maybe. Today, I want you right where you are."

I whisper into her ear. "I want this to never fucking end."

She moans. "Mmmmm."

I'm so close to coming that I slow down. Then stop.

"Why are you stopping?"

"I'm going to explode if I don't stop." I hold her ass with my hands as I catch my breath, and then guide my cock back inside her, and I slow the pace to feel every sensation, every quiver, every corner of that smooth, miraculous place. She soon decides to resume the pace we had earlier and begins bouncing back on my dick, and I become dizzy, high, feeling everything.

I feel that if I speed up and turn up the intensity even more, she will get closer to orgasm. I pick up the tempo of my thrusts and reach around and touch her, stimulating her to the edge of orgasm.

And then *she* stops. "Jack, I want us facing each other." She rolls onto her back and looks into my eyes. And I gaze at her and realize that now we will make love. I understand that it is impossible not to love her when we are face to face. In a moment her gorgeous legs are wrapped around me. Smiling, she looks into my eyes.

"Promise me you will always look at me this way… when I'm inside you."

"Promise. Cross my heart, Jack."

The intensity of our love and lovemaking is almost shocking. And our kissing is at turns gentle, tender, passionate, and all-consuming.

"Oh Jack, don't stop…don't stop. God, don't you ever stop. Ahhhh!"

And I explode. Moaning, I pull out and see that the condom is full. Anna reaches out to me and pulls off the condom, dropping it to the floor. Smiling up at me, she slowly strokes me and coxes another orgasm. I kiss her deeply and then go down, nibbling her neck. My tongue traces a path between her breasts, over the belly button, and to her center, where she is soaking wet and her hands pull my face into heaven.

We take a very long shower together, kissing and slathering and touching until the water goes cold.

Later we go to dinner at a Mexican restaurant.

We are handed menus, but she pushes hers away. "I'm just gonna watch you eat. Well, maybe some chips and queso and ice water."

"You're not going to eat?"

"I'll have something later."

I order a burrito, chips and queso, and a margarita. We hold hands. I look at her beautiful face, her mouth.

The margarita is amazing. My burrito arrives, and it's huge.

"You have a big appetite," she says.

I look at her and smile. "You have no idea. But listen, why not eat something more substantial. Or have some of this?"

"Okay. I will have some burrito." And she takes several bites. "It's good, Jack."

"Anna, if you found, say, sixty thousand dollars in your attic, what would you do with it? Assuming that you were not behind on bills or needed a new car. Would you start a business? Buy something? New appliances?"

"Hmm. Found money. Interesting question. I know so many people who need, like, fifty or a hundred dollars to get back on their feet. My mom, for example, wants me to loan her fourteen hundred dollars so that she can buy a reliable car for work. She would absolutely pay me back. But I don't have it. I have a friend who needs to see a dentist. A coworker at Walmart needs to get caught up on her electric bill. I think I would use it to help people who need a boost. And maybe I would get myself a knew winter coat or shoes."

"I like that," I say.

We head to karaoke after dinner. And immediately Anna is ready to sing. She sings "I Will Remember You" by Amy Grant. And she gets a standing ovation. She sings another and I am suddenly in love with that voice.

We go back to my house, where she stands in my kitchen and eats ice cream. We kiss.

"Jack, can I see the rest of the email?" she says.

I just stare at her.

"Jack?"

"Well, yes. I guess. It's top secret, you know. You can't tell anyone. If you mentioned it to the wrong person, it could get both of us in trouble."

"Jack, I promise."

I go to my office, grab a folder, and return to the kitchen, where Anna is now eating a banana.

I open the folder and hand her the seven pages. She begins to read.

"Belinda Carlisle?" she asks, then giggles.

"It was a long time ago," I say.

She continues to read.

"You were a player, huh?" she says. "Maybe you still are. And a peeping Tom."

"Well…"

"'Do not get remarried in 2009 or in any year that starts with a 2,'" she reads out loud. "'Some men are not meant to be husbands.'" She looks up at me. "Who are you? Really?"

"Just read the rest before you start making—"

"I'm such a fool." She drops the papers on the floor.

"You have not read far enough."

"I don't care." And she walks out of the kitchen and out the back door. I can see her heading to her car. And before I decide what to do, she is gone.

Chapter Twenty-Two

November 12, 2003

I HAVE BEEN TEXTING, calling, and emailing Anna every day. No response. Also, I've been working on my house every day. For the past seven days I have done a ton of work in the sunroom on the second floor. Joy and Envie have helped me paint walls and assemble furniture. We've gone shopping. We bought throw rugs, sheets, bath towels, and a lot more.

I call Anna's phone. It goes to voicemail as usual. But this time I leave a message.

"Anna, it's Jack. Please stop by my house today. I want you to read the entire email. I think you need to know everything that is in that letter. And then we can talk about it. Or you can walk away. Your choice. But until you read the email, I won't be able to let you go. I won't be able to move on." I pause. "I'll be here all day."

I continue to work on the house. I sand floors for two hours. Then I stow my tools and take a shower.

I get dressed, grab a beer, and head to the front door. As I'm sitting on the front porch, I see her Jeep pull up to the curb. Her parking is okay.

She walks into the front yard. "Hi, Jack. How are you?"

"I miss you."

"Okay. So show me the email."

I bring it out to the porch and she reads. Silently. So silently. She finishes reading and sets the pages on her lap.

"Please, let's talk about the letter," I say. "Yes, I was a player. Maybe I still am. I have loved deeply and lost profoundly. I've learned to keep things casual. I chose to chase excitement and passion and then break it off before anyone got hurt, but that hasn't worked out so good. I still hurt people. But this feels different, Anna. You are generous, and sweet, and creative, and smart, and so fucking gorgeous. In the alternate timeline you asked me to leave. And I did. And neither one of us understood what the other was feeling. But now I do. You do."

Anna looks at me.

"Anna, you're more than I deserve, and maybe always will be, because I have so much growing to do. But I will spend the rest of my life trying to be the best version of me and the man you deserve. I know that we love each other now and can love each other twenty years from now."

"I believe you, Jack. I adore the way you look at me.

And I want you to look at me like that for a very long time."

And we kiss.

"Are you going to make me figure out the anagram?" she says.

"Which one? There are four in the email. At one point in the email, Jack writes: 'Do you remember when Dad would check out a passerby and say, "Get back to yes"?' Well, 'check out a passerby' translates to 'purchase eBay stock,' and 'get back to yes' is 'get eBay stock.' So I have been buying stock. Slowly. Then he writes, 'By the way, in 2009, please make sure Dad does not buy that Uncle Moose car.' I don't have an Uncle Moose. It's nonsense. So I spent days moving Scrabble tiles around. And it appeared: CANCEROUS MOLE. Apparently, Jack was forbidden to tell me to get Dad to see a dermatologist in 2009."

"And the last one?"

"In the story about Jack seeing you in Colorado, Anna tells him that in 2009 she got a thank-you card: 'Ms. Connor, Thank you for your $5 donation to the Down Syndrome Association. Sincerely, Mr. Billy E. Mouere.' So 'Mr. Billy E. Mouere' is an anagram for 'I'll remember you.'"

"So in 2009, Jack wanted to tell me his feelings without getting me in trouble with Tom."

"Yes."

Anna asks, "Were you really involved in the Nine Eleven stuff?"

"Yeah. It's over, I think. I kept just one person from flying that day. So the people who wanted to change the timeline might have to start over and send another email to someone else. I don't know. One man I contacted had promised to stay off that flight, but he never canceled his reservation. The newspapers are saying he's a hero. Todd Beamer had called his wife during the flight and was told that the plane was doomed. She told her husband that the hijackers likely were going to crash it into the White House. So apparently Beamer and others decided to overpower the terrorists. And they succeeded."

"That's crazy. Why would you be told to keep heroes off the plane?"

"I have no idea."

Anna then said, "What was in the bathroom in the office building?"

"Sixty thousand dollars. In ones. It's a long story. But later, I was afraid that someone involved in the mission might be dispatched to take it from me because I screwed up the Nine Eleven assignment. But I still have it all—well, I have around fifty-six thousand dollars left. I was actually more concerned that they might try to keep us apart. But that fear is mostly gone now."

"Jack—"

"Would you come inside for a minute. I want to show you something."

"Okay, Jack."

I lead Anna upstairs, down a hall, past the bathroom, through Envie's room, to the sunroom.

"Surprise!" I say.

Anna stops and looks around the room. "Jack. It's a nursery. It's beautiful."

"The girls helped me decorate and shop for curtains and furniture. They know about you. I haven't told them everything, of course. But they are excited. And hopeful."

"Hopeful?"

"Hopeful that you and the baby will move in. That we can be a family."

Chapter Twenty-Three

November 22, 2003

ANNA AND I TALK by phone every day for several days.

Anna tells me that she wants to visit her mom around Christmas. Her mom is in Springfield, Missouri.

Instead of staying with her mom, who smokes indoors (and billows smoke like the steel mills in Granite City), Anna will be staying at a Hampden Inn a few miles from her mom's house. And I intend to meet her there on Thursday, December 23, 2003.

And of course the email comes.

Subject: I told you to back off

Hey asshole, I told you to stay away from Anna. She's my fiancée and you have overstepped. I will find you.

. . .

I don't respond. But in my opinion, she is no longer anyone's fiancée. Not even mine.

Whether he is serious about finding me, I'm not sure. I doubt he cares enough about Anna to drive to Missouri to kick my ass.

Chapter Twenty-Four

December 23, 2003

IT'S LIGHTLY SNOWING. And it is starting to feel like Christmas.

I arrive at the Hampden Inn on Glenstone at five p.m. I see Anna's Jeep around the back near the dumpsters, and I park a few spaces away. Her text says that she's in room 209. I have a surprise for Anna. So I untie it and carry it into the hotel.

She answers the door in a Hampden Inn white bathrobe. *OMG.*

"Hey, you!" I say. "Getting ready for a shower?"

"No." She pauses, staring at what's in my hands. "You brought a Christmas tree? Into a hotel? Why didn't they stop you?"

"I don't know. The guy at the front desk just shook his head. Maybe it's not so unusual."

She motions for me to enter and I do. She closes and

locks the door. I set the tree against the wall. We can decorate it later.

"Okay," I say. "I'm not in Springfield often, but there's a great restaurant downtown called Civil. I can drive us there. The gooey butter cake ice cream sandwiches are to die for. So put on a pretty dress—"

"Jack, engaging in flirty conversation and a wearing pretty dress at dinner to get your attention are not what I want to do today. So I've decided to be honest with you." She unties the robe and lets it fall to the floor. She's nude. Not even a thong. And those curves. It's like I'm in the presence of a pin-up model. A pin-up girl with a four-and-a-half-month baby bump. She then steps toward me and puts a hand on my face. Her other hand is tracing a vertical line along my oxford shirt, touching each button. "I want you to really see me. I want you to touch me, taste me, take me. I need you to satisfy the ache inside me. The ache between my legs. And I need that now."

"I'm glad you are being honest," I say. And I pull her into my arms and kiss her. "Flirty and dressed in pretty clothes are features I can resist. Nude and sexy and in my arms… Well, that's another story. I predict that I'll be naked in less than five minutes."

And I am.

Anna visits her mom for several hours a day for the next two days. She says that introducing me to her mom is complicated by the fact that her mom thinks Anna will reconcile with Tom. That she *should* reconcile with him. But Anna is mine now.

On Christmas Eve we go to a nearby café with her guitar. She says she has a surprise for me.

She places a chair near the fireplace, and the owner brings out a microphone and small speaker.

"Hi, everyone. I'm Anna. I don't play or sing here often, but I see some familiar faces. Normally I sing covers. But tonight I want to do an original song for my love, Jack. It's called 'This Time.'"

Anna sits and strums her guitar, and so begins a beautiful ballad. I sit nearby and watch this beauty sing.

I like lying here just to touch your body
Make you laugh and make you smile
Just make love to you a while
You can keep me here just by sayin', 'Stay, baby.'
I'll be right here and do what you say, baby.
'Cause your presence is always my favorite present

I just wanna watch you move
And help you get your groove… on
'Cause we now have a second chance
And this time, I don't wanna lose this bliss
And even though I have you now
Sometimes fate can step in anyhow
And I'd never get over …
So this time, we won't forget this kiss

God, I want you to be mine

And not just on your mind
'Cause I now see a future
Where dismal days are fewer
But even though I have you now
I can't count on forever anyhow
And I'll never want to be without…
So this time, we'll forge the future

This time, I won't let you go without a fight
It's in this time when I'll be with you tonight.

She stands and says, "Merry Christmas, everyone. And Merry Christmas, Jack. I love you."

Christmas Day we wake early and exchange presents. We make love and then lie in bed.

"Anna, do you believe in God?" I say.

"Yes. He must exist because I've been angry with God since the day my father died, nine years ago. How can I be angry with a God that doesn't exist?" She pauses. "Dad had a stroke while at work. Died the next day."

"Maybe you and God can reconcile when you are holding a baby in your arms."

"Yeah."

I leave for St. Louis at noon so that I can spend time with my daughters.

Chapter Twenty-Five

May 2, 2004

ANNA IS COMPLETELY NUDE in the birth pool, which is in our bedroom. I am fully clothed and sitting on the floor, trying to hold her, soothe her, as the contractions come closer together.

Our midwife, Ellen, says, "Anna, you are getting very close."

"I feel the need to push. Is that okay," says Anna.

"Push for six seconds, dear."

Anna bears down and cries out.

And there she is, emerging into the world. Anna begins to cry or laugh or both. And she slowly sits up, her breasts now above water, glistening. Anna gently brings this new life to the surface and she rests on Mom, skin to skin, now taking her first breaths.

The midwife kneels next to Anna, making sure the nose is clear. "She's a healthy one, she is."

I am amazed and can't seem to speak. "She's beautiful," I whisper.

Later, when the midwife has gone and Anna is asleep, I hold her. And I realize that I'm already very attached.

"Hey, you," I whisper. "I love you. And I love your mom too."

Epilogue

January 10, 2027

ARMY BASE, LEXINGTON, KENTUCKY

"Sir, a reporter found a safe buried beneath a pine tree in Maryland Heights, Missouri. Inside was three thousand dollars in cash and a journal that appears to prove that the temporal distortion email program works. The reporter is convinced that the journal is authentic. It was found in the backyard of a house that the subject owned from 1993 to 1999. It was buried about three feet down and appears to be about twenty years old. We have a copy of the email that was inside. The journal has entries from 2000 to 2009 and mentions some of the actions taken with respect to Anna Connor and a bank heist. There are some photos of children and newspaper clippings that are from September 2001. Clearly, the mission was successful. However, all personnel who had been part of the operation are suffering from amnesia and panic attacks."

"Thank you, Sergeant. What is the status of the reporter?"

"Sir, he has been detained. We have confiscated all documents and the cash. If he cooperates, he may be released this week."

"Have you located O'Donnell?"

"We did. He and Anna Connor were living together in Chicago. But O'Donnell was living under an alias. Says he received an email on December 31, 1999, from the future. He mostly followed the instructions he was given but admits he did eventually contact a reporter about the mission because he came to believe that he was manipulated."

"What can you tell me about the clippings?"

"*St. Louis Post-Dispatch* mostly. September twelfth to thirtieth, 2001. Clippings about the Nine Eleven attacks in New York and Washington. The flight that crashed in Pennsylvania. We know O'Donnell was told do something to affect the outcome of events that day. According to the subject and the email from the capsule, he was told to keep two people off Flight 93. But one of the passengers decided to fly anyway. So when Flight 93 crashed, forty-three passengers and crew were killed instead of forty-four. Mark Bingham has stated in published reports that someone paid him hundreds of dollars to change airlines that day."

"Sergeant, the president wants to be briefed on all of it. She wants to be briefed ASAP."

About the Author

M. S. McConnell is a freelance copy editor in Saint Charles, Missouri.

Acknowledgments

Deb, my wife, thank you for joy and love and letting me hole up to write. I love you.

Daughters Kat, Emily, Mary, Amanda, and Joy, thank you for prodding me to do more than stare at the laptop.

Toni Feldhaus, thank you for reading the first, very rough draft.

Kent Sanders, you gave me the confidence to finish this project and the discipline to be a daily writer. Thank you.

Christine McConnell, Micheal Woodruff, and Red, thank you for the honest feedback.

Courtney Andersson, thank you for the editing work. You are amazing.

Kristi, thank you for your wonderful work on the cover.

M. J. James, thank you so much for the interior design.

Made in the USA
Monee, IL
13 November 2024

69902714R00100